Have you got them all?

A Note from Enid Blyton's Daughter

Dear Readers,

Enid Blyton wrote *The Naughtiest Girl In The School* when I was eight years old and it has always been one of my favourites. It appeared as a serial in Enid Blyton's little magazine called *Sunny Stories*, which came out every Friday. My friends and I would have to wait a whole week before the next chapter came out. It was the first school story that Enid Blyton had written and I longer for the proper book to be published.

Enid Blyton was not only a writer for children, she was also involved in the editing and writing of books for teachers. She was a trained Froebel and Montessori teacher and had run her own school before she married.

She was very interested in the world of education and especially a mixed boarding school called Summerfields, which was opened by A. S. Neill in 1923. He believed that the school should be governed by the children themselves with the teachers only taking part if asked to by the children.

In the *Naughtiest Girl* series, Whyteleafe School is run in the same way with a meeting held every week in the school hall. The head boy and girl presided over the meeting aided by twelve monitors chosen by the other children. It was a kind of school

Parliament, where the children made their own rules, heard grumbles and complaints, judged one another and punished bad behaviour. All problems were discussed and decided by the children and only in very difficult situations were the head teachers asked for their advice.

Of all the school series this is my favourite. The way the school is run has always made me more interested in the characters, and I think, adds to the excitement of the story. I hope you enjoy reading them.

With love from *Gillian*

The further adventures of Enid Blyton's
Naughtiest Girl

The Naughtiest Girl marches On

Anne Digby

Hodder
Children's
Books

A division of Hachette Children's Books

First published in Great Britain in 1999
by Hodder Children's Books
This edition published in 2007

For further information on Enid Blyton, please contact
www.blyton.com

1

A Catalogue record for this book is available from the British Library

ISBN 978 0 340 91780 0

Typeset in Sabon by Avon DataSet Ltd, Bidford-on-Avon, Warks

Printed and bound in Great Britain by Clays Ltd, St Ives plc

The paper and board used in this paperback by Hodder Children's
Books are natural recyclable products made from wood grown in
sustainable forests. The manufacturing processes conform to the
environmental regulations of the country of origin.

Hodder Children's Books
a division of Hachette Children's Books
338 Euston Road, London NW1 3BH
An Hachette Livre UK Company

Contents

1 *Jake is grumpy*

Elizabeth Allen was enjoying life in the second form at Whyteleafe School. By early October she could barely remember what it had felt like to be a first former. How young the new first formers looked now, how small for their age! Surely, she would say in amazement to her best friend Joan, *they'd* never been that small when they were first formers? Joan would smile gently and assure her that a year ago they must have looked every bit as small.

Being a second form monitor with Joan this term made Elizabeth feel all the more grown-up. She was delighted to be a monitor again and refused to let her friend Julian put her off her stride.

'How long will the Naughtiest Girl last this time?' he asked her, an amused light in his green eyes. 'One week? Two weeks? Or till half-term, perhaps?'

'Wait and see, Julian Holland. You might get a surprise. It's exciting being a monitor. Thomas and Emma have got really good ideas. I've not the slightest intention of blotting my copybook!'

It was a long time since Elizabeth really *had* been the school's Naughtiest Girl – but the nickname had stuck. And how Julian loved to tease her about it!

Privately Elizabeth now considered Whyteleafe the best school in the world. She liked the way the pupils made most of the rules themselves, through the weekly Meeting, which was a kind of school parliament. And she loved the monitors' get-togethers that Thomas and Emma, the new head boy and girl, had introduced. All twelve monitors now met Thomas and Emma once a week for tea and biscuits in their study. They helped to plan the main Meeting and were encouraged to put forward ideas. It was known simply as the

Monitors' Meeting, or MM for short.

'Don't forget we've got an MM before tea, Elizabeth!' Joan reminded her friend one day.

They were still outside, after Games. Elizabeth was loitering near the main hockey pitch, where members of the school's first eleven were having a team practice. There were some important matches coming up soon.

'I know, Joan,' replied Elizabeth. 'I'm looking forward to it. Wasn't it good last week?'

There had been three MMs so far and Elizabeth had enjoyed each one. She wanted to play her full part in the smooth running of the school. She was determined to be a dynamic and successful monitor. She took her responsibilities to heart.

'But we haven't got time just to stand around,' Joan said softly. 'We've got to wash and change and smarten up . . .'

'I'm not just standing around, Joan!' Elizabeth pointed out, patiently. 'I'm looking at Jake and his poor ankle, that's all. I'm worried about him, aren't you? We *are* his monitors, after all. I think the least we can do is go over and have a few words with him. He looks so grumpy! Come on, let's try and cheer him up.'

Only then did Joan realize that her friend was gazing not at the team practice but at a forlorn figure sitting on the grass, with his ankle heavily strapped. Joan knew Jake well. He had been in the second form even longer than she had. He was a big, strapping boy for his age. He was a brilliant hockey player and at the end of last season had been selected for the school's first hockey team. He was the youngest pupil ever to have made it into the first eleven. He had played superbly.

'Poor Jake!' she agreed. 'All right, then. But we'd better not talk to him for too long.'

Elizabeth was already striding ahead.

It was sad to see the big boy sitting there, staring miserably into space, while his team-mates practised running and passing and shooting goals. He had returned to school from the summer holidays a different boy, thought Joan. It seemed he had fallen badly on the last day of the holidays and injured his ankle. It had been strapped up for nearly a month now and he was still limping heavily. The injury seemed to have affected his confidence, too. He was much quieter this term than Joan had ever known him.

'Cheer up, Jake!' Elizabeth was telling him, with her bright, friendly smile. 'We just want you to know how proud we are to have a second former who's already in the first hockey team. And already a star! It's such an honour for us. It won't be long now before that ankle of yours is better and it won't be a moment too soon! Mr Warlow says there are some very important matches coming up and the team's not the same without you. We can't wait to see you in action again, I can tell you. The whole second form will be cheering you on from the sidelines!'

Even at the best of times, Jake was the strong, silent sort of boy. He seemed taken aback by such effusiveness. His cheeks turned red.

'Oh, leave off, Elizabeth,' he said grumpily.

'Don't be embarrassed, Jake!' said Joan, tactfully. 'We just want you to know that our thoughts are with you. It's such a shame for you, not being able to play games. We do hope the ankle will be better soon.'

'Thanks, Joan,' mumbled the big boy.

'It's *got* to be!' declared Elizabeth, in her boisterous way. 'I am going to wish and wish and WISH your ankle to get better, Jake! Just you wait and see!'

The boy shrugged and made no response.

'Come on, Elizabeth. We must dash now!' Joan tugged at Elizabeth's arm. 'We mustn't be late for the MM!'

As they went indoors, Elizabeth sighed. She'd hoped to cheer Jake up but instead she seemed to have made him grumpier than ever!

'He seemed surprised at my coming over and talking to him,' she frowned. 'I got the impression that he'd quite forgotten I'm one of his monitors this term.'

'He probably had,' laughed Joan.

'Do you think it would be a good idea if all monitors had a special armband?' continued Elizabeth. 'Shall we bring it up at the MM and see what Thomas and Emma say?'

'Don't be hasty, Elizabeth,' replied Joan. 'We can't bring ideas up just to please ourselves. We go to the MM as representatives of form two. We'd need to find out what lots of other people in the form think about it first – and there isn't time.'

'Here come Kathleen and Jenny!' exclaimed Elizabeth. 'We can ask them what they think while we're getting ready.'

The four girls shared dormitory number 14, a big sunny room on the first floor. As Elizabeth and Joan prepared to go to the Monitors' Meeting, they talked to the other two about the armband idea.

'Do you think we really need monitors to have an armband?' said Kathleen, her cheeks rosier than ever after an hour on the games field. 'Everybody knows who they are.'

'I'm not sure they always do,' pouted Elizabeth.

'It's a good idea in some ways,' reflected Jenny. 'But it would mean the school having to spend money to get them made. The Beauty and the Beast might think it's a waste of money!'

Miss Belle and Miss Best were the joint headmistresses. They weren't greatly in favour of unnecessary fripperies and frills.

'We could make our own,' suggested Elizabeth.

By the time she had finished chattering and brushing her hair and (at Joan's suggestion) sponging a jam mark off her school skirt, it was getting late. The two friends hurried off along the corridor to go to the meeting – and bumped straight into Julian.

He had come looking for Elizabeth. He was still wearing his tracksuit after Games and was disappointed to see her looking so smartly dressed.

'Oh, why have you changed, Elizabeth?

We were planning to go for a pony ride before tea!'

Elizabeth's hand flew to her mouth.

'Oh, Julian, sorry! How awful of me. I forgot I had an MM today. Can we go for a ride tomorrow, instead? But, listen, there's an idea I want to tell you about. I need to know your opinion . . .'

At that moment, two other second form boys appeared.

'Harry . . . Martin . . . I need your opinions, as well.'

Elizabeth stood there in the corridor and declaimed her idea about the special armbands for school monitors. Joan looked anxiously at her watch.

'Well, Julian, what do you think?' ended Elizabeth.

Her friend threw back his head and roared with laughter.

'What a horrible idea, Elizabeth! Do you want to be mistaken for a member of the secret police or something?'

Harry and Martin started tittering. Elizabeth . . . armband . . . secret police. What a joke!

'All right, all right. I was only asking!' protested Elizabeth.

She suddenly went off the idea, herself. It had fallen flat. All the fizz had gone out of it. Although she hated being teased by Julian, she always valued his opinion. By the time the two girls had reached the door of Thomas and Emma's big study, her mind was made up.

'I don't think we'd better say anything about the armband idea, Joan,' whispered Elizabeth. 'It doesn't seem to have a lot of support.'

Joan murmured her agreement.

Privately, she was thinking about Jake. It might have slipped the big boy's mind that Elizabeth was one of his monitors but how could he have escaped the fact? Elizabeth was so keen! She was so determined to be a successful and dynamic monitor. There was really no need for her to think about wearing an armband!

It was much more likely, reasoned Joan, that

the boy was upset at being reminded about his injury, by a monitor or anybody else, no matter how kindly meant. It only made him more grumpy. Elizabeth had better go easy in that quarter, she thought.

Out loud, she simply said:

'I expect there will be a lot of other things to talk about.'

'Yes!' replied Elizabeth eagerly. 'I wonder what Thomas and Emma have got in store for us to discuss this week? I expect it will be something interesting!'

2 Thomas and Emma air a new idea

'Hello, Elizabeth! Hello, Joan!' The head girl ushered them in with a smile. 'You'd better grab your tea and biscuits before you sit down. We're all crammed together like sardines as usual.'

'Sorry we're a bit late, Emma!' apologized Elizabeth.

The study was packed. The two friends had to squeeze past all the other boys and girls to get to the table where their mugs of tea awaited them. The mugs stood next to a plate of biscuits. Elizabeth chose her biscuits with care – a shortbread and a chocolate digestive.

'If you can *find* anywhere to sit down!' laughed Thomas. The tall, fair-haired boy was standing by the window, waiting to start. 'Last to arrive had better sit on the floor if they can't find anywhere else!'

Joan managed to find a perch on the arm of a chintz-covered armchair normally reserved for visitors. Then Donald stood up and insisted on giving Elizabeth his place on a wooden bench that had been brought in.

'I'll sit on the floor next to Peter,' smiled the older boy. 'I don't mind at all. Budge up a bit, Peter.'

Peter was the youngest there. He had gone up from the junior class to the first form this term and had been made a monitor.

Elizabeth sandwiched herself on to the bench between Eileen and Richard, who were also monitors now. What fun these get-togethers were, she decided. She sipped her tea slowly and gazed round the room. All twelve monitors had turned up, as in previous weeks.

Whereas the main Meeting in the school hall each week was a formal affair, these little MMs were just the reverse, everybody squashed into a small space, the atmosphere relaxed and jolly.

'Thank you all for coming!' began Thomas. 'I see we've got a full house, as usual. And that's good because Emma and I want to give something an airing. It's a completely new idea. We need to know whether you like it yourselves – and whether you think your classmates would approve. Emma – you explain the thinking behind it.'

Emma finished her tea, placed the cup down and swung round in her chair to face them all.

'Tom and I were talking the other day about how we all like to win honours. It's part of human nature. If we're good at games, we try to get into the teams. And if we're good at lessons, we try to come top in class. However some boys and girls are not especially good at games or brainy either but they may have other fine qualities. We thought, is there a way *they* can be given recognition at Whyteleafe too? Some honour they can compete for on equal terms? What do you think?'

The monitors received the idea with enthusiasm.

'You mean, people who do something unselfish?' asked young Peter.

'A noble deed?' exclaimed Elizabeth, eagerly.

'An act of bravery?' suggested Donald.

'Exactly!' said Emma, pleased to see how quickly the monitors were warming to the idea. 'All of those things. Hands up all of you who think such a prize would be popular with the boys and girls in your form.'

At once every hand in the room shot up.

Thomas smiled as he looked round at the forest of hands.

'Good!' he said. 'In that case, Emma and I would like to announce the plan at this week's Meeting. Let's work out the details. How often should we give out the honour? Perhaps once a term, do you think?'

'Yes! And keep it separate, so award it at half-term!' suggested Eileen.

'But what will the honour be called, Thomas?' asked Donald.

'Now, there's a good question,' smiled Thomas. 'Let's put our thinking caps on.'

After that, the discussion raged for several minutes. Elizabeth was aglow. She liked the head boy and girl's idea. Now they were all being asked to think of the name for the new honour. It was so exciting to be in at the very beginning of things like this. A new tradition at Whyteleafe School . . .

Suggested names for the honour came thick and fast.

'The Bravery Award!'

'The Gold Star for Good Conduct!'

'No – the Gold Star for Courage . . .'

'What about the Good Deed Award?'

In the end, it was one of the fourth form monitors, Eric, who came up with the best name. He was a thoughtful, learned-looking boy. He got to his feet, adjusted his spectacles and cleared his throat.

'May I say something? I'll never forget some of the things that William and Rita told us about courage at camp last term. They knew the true meaning of courage, didn't they? And they explained it so well. I'm sure the whole school would wish to remember them.'

'They were the finest head boy and girl that any school could hope for,' said Thomas, humbly. 'Emma and I are going to have to work hard to live up to their example.'

Emma nodded, her eyes misting over.

'And so, Eric?' she asked.

Before Eric could reply, Elizabeth suddenly guessed what he was going to say. A thrill ran through her and she clapped her hands. She couldn't stop herself, shouting it out loud –

'The William and Rita Award!' she cried. 'That's what you're going to say, isn't it, Eric?'

'Yes! That's it, exactly. You've taken the words right out of my mouth, Elizabeth!'

There were surprised gasps all round and then everyone began to cheer. The William and Rita Award. Excellent!

Thomas and Emma looked at each other in delight.

'That's a lovely name for the honour, Eric,' smiled Emma. 'Quite brilliant.'

'Perfect!' exclaimed Thomas.

And the whole room agreed.

It turned into a long session after that. There was so much to discuss! But it was all very fruitful. By the end of the session, not only had the name of the award been decided but so had all the details of how the winner would be selected. These would be announced in full at the school Meeting.

'Until then, this is all hush-hush,' Emma reminded them. She placed a finger to her lips. 'Not a word to anyone. We don't want this leaking out in dribs and drabs. It must be announced in the proper way when the whole school is assembled.'

Elizabeth and Joan were used to this. Things that the monitors discussed at MMs often had to remain confidential, until the head boy and girl were ready to make them public.

'It's so lucky that we're friends, Joan!' remarked Elizabeth, as they went into the dining-hall for tea. 'We can talk to each other as much as we like about things that are said at the MMs. I'd die if I couldn't talk to somebody about them! I wonder who'll get the first William and Rita Award? I wonder if it will be anyone in our form? Wouldn't that be an honour!'

She was still bubbling over with it all when she sat down for tea. Julian had saved her a place by the window, at one of the second form tables.

'Hello, Elizabeth!' Julian wore his usual grin. 'How did the meeting of the secret police go, then? What are you looking so excited about? Did you decide anything interesting?'

'As a matter of fact, we did,' Elizabeth blurted out.

'What then?'

'It'll be announced at the school Meeting,' said Elizabeth. 'But my lips are sealed till then. Oh, sorry, Julian. I shouldn't have said anything, should I?'

A look of annoyance had crossed her friend's face.

'It's not *my* fault,' she added. 'It's a rule!'

'Since when has the Naughtiest Girl worried

her head about rules?' asked Julian, waspishly. 'If this monitor business is going to turn you into the school goody-goody, I will feel very badly let down, Elizabeth Allen.'

'Sorry, Julian,' Elizabeth repeated.

Then he gave her hair a friendly tweak and smiled.

'Only joking,' he said airily. 'No leaks allowed from the Cabinet Office, eh? Has to be announced at the full sitting of parliament? Fair enough.'

Daniel Carter, sitting opposite, was looking solemn.

'Julian, Elizabeth would love to tell you what happened. You can see that just by looking at her face! I'm sure she *would*, if she could. Gosh, I can't wait for the Meeting, to hear what it is. I wish I'd been at the MM, Elizabeth. They *do* sound fun.'

The wistful expression on Daniel's face gave Elizabeth a sudden pang.

For the first few days of term, Daniel had been appointed as a form monitor in Elizabeth's place, while she had been in disgrace about something. But as soon as Elizabeth had been vindicated, the boy had of course stood down to enable her to have her monitorship back. Poor Daniel!

But before Elizabeth could brood about it, another boy called down the table to her. It was Julian's cousin, Patrick. The two cousins liked to keep their distance as they did not get on particularly well.

'Please stop gabbing, Elizabeth, and pass the bread rolls up this end! I'm starving! I've been practising my ping-pong for the last hour!'

Elizabeth smiled and passed the bread basket along the table.

Patrick smiled back.

'Don't forget it's squad practice tomorrow,' he reminded her. 'I'm going to beat you for a change!'

They were both in the school table-tennis squad but Patrick was only the team's first reserve. He was a very competitive boy and was striving with all his might to become a full team member, like Elizabeth.

'You *wish*, Patrick!' Elizabeth called back cheerfully.

After that, she tucked into her tea with gusto.

She gave no further thought to Daniel's comments, nor Julian's. It would be some days before she would have good reason to recall them.

3   *Elizabeth hears about a brave deed*

The table-tennis practice, the one that Patrick had mentioned, took place after lessons the following day. Mr Warlow, the sports master, had asked all team members and team reserves to attend. He and Emma, who was table-tennis captain, wanted to check that everyone was in good form for a match on Saturday. It would be an away match against Hickling Green School, their old rivals, to take place alongside a hockey fixture. Hickling Green had a very strong hockey eleven. Mr Warlow feared that Whyteleafe might do badly in the hockey match, especially with Jake out of the team. But he had high hopes of his table-tennis squad! It was a good one this term.

Elizabeth would not have been allowed to miss the practice, even if she'd wanted to. And, of course, she would not have dreamt of missing it. She was looking forward to the trip on Saturday. Miss Belle and Miss Best had hired a full-size coach to accommodate both teams and their supporters. It would be so exciting if they could beat their old rivals, thought Elizabeth, and they would be sure to get a lovely tea afterwards.

However it was a great disappointment to have to put off going riding with Julian for the second day running.

'Don't worry, Elizabeth, it's not your fault,' he said, good-humouredly. 'It's just a pity we're not allowed to go riding after tea this term, with the evenings drawing in. I'll fix up a ride with Robert, instead.'

'Let's go and feed the ponies after tea. At least we're allowed to do that!' suggested Elizabeth. 'I haven't seen them for days and I'm missing them.'

'Good!' said Julian. 'I like that idea. Off you

go to your ping-pong, then. Don't wear yourself out. See you at tea!'

It was a busy practice session. Emma and Mr Warlow spent most of the time coaching the boys and girls. They were shown how to improve their footwork, as well as their batting technique. They were then split up to play a proper practice game, paired according to ability. Elizabeth was asked to play against Patrick. The two were evenly matched although Elizabeth was considered to have the edge.

She usually beat Patrick. But today he was determined to reverse that situation. He had been working on his game furiously, for days.

And he knew that both Emma and the teacher were keeping a watchful eye on all three tables, checking everybody's current form. It made him very focused.

But Elizabeth was equally aware that they were being kept an eye on. And she was very focused, too.

They both played exceptionally well.

Patrick served first and took the lead, 3–2. Then Elizabeth served and lost only one of her service points to lead 6–4. After that the lead passed from one to the other, backwards and forwards, the scores tending to go with service. The rallies were long, fast and furious.

The score reached 20–20!

Now they had to change service on every point. The first to lead by two clear points would win the game. In the tension of the moment, Patrick's service faltered. It twice missed the table and he lost the point. 21–20 to Elizabeth. Then Elizabeth did a safe medium-paced service, nothing fancy. Patrick returned to her backhand. She gave back a spinning lob that just caught the edge of the table. Patrick had to swoop low and only just managed to return it.

It was a weak, loopy return. It bounced high on Elizabeth's side of the table. She changed to forehand grip, swung her arm back and then—

Whooosh!

A beautiful forehand smash to the far corner!

Patrick dived . . . too late. He missed.

'22–20!' Elizabeth cried in delight. 'I've won! I've won!'

The ping-pong ball hit the far wall and came rolling slowly back towards Patrick's foot. In his fury and frustration, and in the heat of the moment, he stamped on it.

Crunch!

The ping-pong ball was flattened.

The sudden sound made Emma glance round.

'Oh, Patrick, you clumsy boy! You've trodden on the ball!'

Already regretting his temper, Patrick stared at Elizabeth imploringly. He was silently begging her not to give him away! She was the only person who had seen him deliberately stamp on the ball.

Emma was scooping the poor ball up from the floor, examining it.

'It's past repair, I'm afraid,' she said.

'Oh, what a shame,' said Elizabeth, innocently.

'I'll replace it, Emma,' Patrick said, quickly. 'I'll go to the village and buy a new one with my own money. I'll go straight away if you like. Has the session ended now?'

'Oh, Patrick, you are a good sport,' said Emma. 'Will you really? As a matter of fact, we're getting rather low on balls at the moment. Would you like to go with him, please, Elizabeth? You've both got some time before tea.'

At Whyteleafe School, pupils were allowed to go down to the village. But it was a strict rule that they went out in pairs and not on their own.

'The sun's coming out!' said Elizabeth cheerfully. 'I'll be glad of a walk to the village.'

As the boy and girl strolled out through the school gates and along the quiet road to the village Patrick looked sullen and shamefaced.

'Thanks for not giving me away, Elizabeth,' he said.

Elizabeth felt slightly sorry for him.

'Cheer up,' she said. 'I've got an awfully hot

temper myself, so I know just what it's like to lose it!'

Patrick did not reply. The fact was that, in spite of their occasional clashes, he could not help liking and admiring Elizabeth. He often wished that she would like and admire *him*. It was annoying the way she seemed so much to prefer his cousin Julian. And now he felt angry with himself for losing his temper like that. It had been childish.

'It's all right for you to lose your temper, Elizabeth,' he said. 'You're only a girl.'

Elizabeth couldn't help smiling to herself. It was a typical Patrick remark – and just one of the reasons why she much preferred his cousin Julian!

Patrick did not speak again until they reached the shop.

'The truth is, Elizabeth,' he confessed, as they stared in the shop window, 'that I really thought I might beat you today. You've been so busy with this monitor business. You haven't been practising so much lately. I was so hoping that they'd notice me. How well I was playing . . . Then maybe I'd get a chance to play in a match soon.'

'You *were* playing well, Patrick,' said Elizabeth, truthfully. 'And the game could easily have gone the other way. And I'm sure they did notice you and that you'll be given a chance, sooner or later.'

A little bell on the shop door tinkled softly as they pushed it open and went inside. It was a lovely, old-fashioned shop with a warm musky smell. The table-tennis balls were in a cardboard box, jammed between the shuttlecocks and the birthday cards.

Patrick picked out a shiny new white ping-pong ball, took it to the counter and paid for it. Elizabeth followed him out of the shop.

They stood outside on the pavement wondering whether there was time to go across to the sweet shop, on the opposite side of the road. They decided there was not.

Then suddenly a car squealed to a halt in front of them and a mother burst out of the car, with a small red-headed child. They seemed to be in a great state of excitement. They were looking this way.

Something strange was going on.

The little girl was pointing at Patrick! She was whispering to her mother. Her eyes were very big and round. Her cheeks had gone very pink.

'Are you *sure*, Sandra?' the woman kept asking. 'Are you really sure it was him?'

'Yes, Mummy. It was, it was, it was!'

'Look at his face. You are quite sure?'

'Sure as sure can be, Mummy!' squeaked the child, getting more excited by the minute. 'Cross my heart. It was him!'

Then an extraordinary thing happened. To Elizabeth's amazement, the woman ran up to Patrick and embraced him! There were tears of emotion in her eyes.

'Thank you!' she exclaimed. 'Thank you for saving my little Sandra's life! Every day when we come to the shops, I tell Sandra to look out for you, in case she should see you again. We so wanted to be able to thank you!'

Patrick stood there, blushing.

And then the woman picked the child up and thrust her at Patrick.

'Give the young man a kiss, Sandra. Tell him you're sorry for being such a silly girl and giving us all a fright. Say thank you, nicely.'

Patrick's blushing increased tenfold as the little girl planted a kiss on his cheek and lisped her thank-yous.

The woman then set the child down on the pavement and turned to speak to Elizabeth.

'I don't suppose your friend's ever told you he's a hero?'

'No!' exclaimed Elizabeth. 'Whatever happened?'

'My Sandra ran out of this shop last week when my back was turned!' the woman explained. 'She ran across the road to go to the sweet shop. That's what happened! And your friend here—' The woman patted Patrick's arm, overcome with emotion. 'There was this car, you see,' she gulped. 'It came speeding round the bend. It didn't see my Sandra. And your friend – he was so brave. He ran into the road and pushed her out of the way, just in time! And he could have been killed himself. And he didn't even stop to let anybody thank him. He just ran off.'

'Patrick!' gasped Elizabeth.

Politely, Patrick bowed to both the mother and child. Then he backed away.

'I'm afraid we're in a bit of a hurry!' he said. 'Come on, Elizabeth.'

He took her arm and marched her swiftly away. Elizabeth could sense the boy's embarrassment. He would never have dreamt, she thought, that his brave deed might come out in this unexpected way. He was walking so fast, he was almost running!

'Thank you again,' the woman called out. 'I just had to stop the car when Sandra saw you. I didn't mean to embarrass you! You're a real hero, young man. I'll never forget you as long as I live!'

Worried that the woman would take

Patrick's discomfiture for rudeness, Elizabeth looked back and gave mother and daughter a friendly wave. Elizabeth's face was flushed with excitement. Her eyes were shining.

'Think nothing of it!' she called. 'It was a pleasure.'

And, as soon as she and Patrick had gone a safe distance, she jerked at his arm and made him halt.

'Patrick! I am absolutely amazed!' she said, gazing at him. 'What a wonderful surprise! I know it's a horrid thing to say but I had no idea that you could be such a brave person. I'm really ashamed of myself now. What a fine thing to do! And to think that when it happened you didn't even wait to be thanked!'

She gazed at him, wide-eyed. She was seeing him in a completely new light.

'Oh, Patrick. I do admire you for this.'

He lowered his gaze, crimson with pleasure.

'Lot of fuss about nothing,' he muttered.

They walked on in silence, each wrapped in their own thoughts. Patrick glanced at

Elizabeth from time to time, as they wandered along. Her lips were parted and there was still that thrilled expression on her face.

She was thinking about the William and Rita Award! Surely, now, no other candidate could possibly match Patrick's claim to it? It was almost as though the very award itself had been designed with Patrick's deed in mind. What an honour for the second form if the very first William and Rita Award came their way!

'What are you thinking about, Elizabeth?' asked Patrick, at length. 'Why are you so quiet?'

They were turning in through the school gates. They could hear a distant bell ringing for tea.

'I'm still thinking about your brave deed, of course. And – Patrick, I can't explain yet – but there's a reason why the whole school is going to need to know about it soon!'

'WHAT?' exclaimed Patrick.

He pulled her to a stop. He gripped her arm. 'Don't you dare, Elizabeth! Nobody's to know about this. *No one*, you understand? You're to promise me at once that you will never say a word to anyone!'

Elizabeth looked at him in dismay. She pouted.

'Why not, Patrick? Why ever not? Quite apart from this – er – special thing, it's right that people should know! I'd like *everybody* to know what you're really like. What a good, brave person you are. And how you've never once showed off about what you did.'

Patrick flushed, basking in Elizabeth's praise.

'Why must I keep it secret, Patrick?' Elizabeth repeated.

The boy thought long and hard, staring at the ground. When he replied, the words were carefully chosen.

'Look at it this way,' he said. 'If a boy in a Whyteleafe uniform was down in the village one day, and performed a brave action, why would nobody know about it? At least one other person should know about it, shouldn't they? I'm not admitting anything and certainly not to a monitor but isn't there a rule at Whyteleafe School? Isn't there a very strict rule that must never be broken?'

'Oh!' gasped Elizabeth. 'Of course! You went down to the village on your own, Patrick! That's it, isn't it? You didn't pair up with somebody else, the way you're supposed to.'

Patrick did not reply. Instead, he let go of Elizabeth's arm and strode on up the school drive.

He looked back over his shoulder.

'Come on, Elizabeth. You're going to be late for tea.'

She hurried after him. She was thinking things over carefully. She caught up with him, outside the doors of the dining-hall.

'Patrick, I can see you're in an awkward situation. But believe me, I'm sure this boy would be forgiven, just this once, for breaking an important school rule. Once everybody knew what a hero he'd been.'

'He's not interested in being a hero, Elizabeth, and that's final. A hero to you, if you like. I don't mind that. But nobody else. So now please shut up about it.'

Swallowing her deep disappointment, Elizabeth went in to tea. Julian and Joan were wondering where she'd got to. Julian's eyebrows raised high upon seeing her enter the dining-hall with Patrick.

They explained how they'd gone down to the shops to buy the new ping-pong ball. Patrick whistled cheerfully and bounced it on the table a few times. Elizabeth watched, admiringly.

Later, when they went to feed the ponies, Julian joked about Patrick.

'Poor Elizabeth. That's what comes of being a monitor. Bad luck!'

Elizabeth would normally have got the point at once and giggled. But today she looked at Julian in surprise.

'Bad luck? What do you mean exactly, Julian?'

'Having to partner Patrick down to the village shop, of course,' he replied, patiently.

'No wonder you looked cross when you got back for tea. Was he a pain, as usual?'

'No, of course not. Patrick's not a pain!'

Julian looked at her in surprise.

'Oh, I know he is sometimes,' Elizabeth added hastily. She drew a deep breath. She must be careful. But she must also come to Patrick's defence. 'Your cousin's quite decent really. He's got hidden depths, you know.'

'Hidden depths?' Julian laughed out loud. 'So well hidden you'd never find them in a million years. Have you gone potty, Elizabeth? Or is this a bad attack of the goody-goody-monitor-itis disease?'

'Of course it isn't, Julian,' retorted Elizabeth, indignantly.

'I think I prefer you when you're being the Naughtiest Girl,' he grinned.

Drat Patrick, thought Elizabeth, not letting her tell anybody about his brave deed! She was longing to tell Julian but her lips had been sealed.

Patrick was pretending it was because he

wanted nobody to find out that he'd been breaking a school rule. But Elizabeth was not convinced about that.

The real reason, she believed, was that, as with any true hero, Patrick was determined that his heroism should go unsung. And, although it made her cross, it also made her admire him all the more for it.

She decided she would try to express her admiration secretly. Somehow she'd find a way to be especially nice to him!

4 An unexpected discovery

With the whole school assembled in the big hall, Thomas and Emma announced the new award. They left it to the very end of Friday's Meeting. Every pupil listened attentively, from the junior children sitting cross-legged on the floor at the front, to the seniors on benches at the back. No boys and girls were allowed to miss the weekly 'parliament'. The joint headmistresses, with Mr Johns, the senior master, sat at the very back of the hall. They were there as observers. They never took part in the Meetings unless, for very difficult matters, their advice was needed.

Elizabeth and Joan sat in chairs on the platform with the other monitors, just behind the head boy and girl. Thomas and Emma sat at a special table, from where they conducted the Meeting.

There had been all the usual business to get through. Money was collected up from pupils who'd received some this week, then given out again to every member of the school in the form of the two pounds weekly allowance. At Whyteleafe School, all money had to be fairly shared. Then 'Special Requests' for extra money were listened to. They were discussed and then either granted or refused. There were no complaints or grumbles to be heard this week but there were several sports announcements. Elizabeth was proud to hear her name read out as a member of the table-tennis team for tomorrow's match against Hickling Green.

Jake's name was again missing from the hockey team list. From her vantage point on the platform, Elizabeth had watched him arrive for the Meeting. His limp, if anything, seemed more pronounced than ever. His ankle was still supported by a thick crepe bandage.

'We are all sorry that Jake will not be able to play for us at Hickling Green tomorrow,' announced Thomas, 'and we take this opportunity to wish him well and hope that his injury is better in time for our next hockey fixture, which will be against Milford Grange.'

Then Emma took over.

'Finally, we have some exciting news to tell you,' she said.

Elizabeth and Joan glanced at each other. At last! They had been waiting eagerly for the moment when the William and Rita Award would be announced. It had been a strain having to keep it secret since the MM. Now the whole school would hear about it. How would it be received? Had the monitors been correct when they'd all voted for it, so sure that their classmates would approve?

They need not have worried. The news was greeted with cheers and applause. It was very well received indeed! Soon a buzz of chatter ran up and down the rows.

A new honour, to be called the William and Rita Award!

To be given not for being brainy or good at games or anything like that but for Outstanding Conduct, such as bravery or unselfishness ... or exceptional kindness. It would be handed out each half-term. What a fantastic idea!

'What are you so quiet for, Patrick?' asked their classmate, Arabella Buckley. 'Don't you like the idea?'

'Just thinking, that's all,' muttered Patrick. He had been listening attentively to the announcement. He appeared to be scowling.

'I think it's an excellent idea,' continued Arabella, primly. She was already trying to work out how she might get to win the new honour. 'The brainy people get paid too much attention around here.'

'What do you think, Julian?' asked Arabella's friend, Rosemary. 'I like the way it's called after William and Rita, don't you?'

'It's a good idea,' conceded Julian. 'And, yes,

it's a good name, too. I'm sure they'd approve!'

Julian glanced up towards the platform, at Elizabeth's glowing face. So this was what the secret had been the other day? He was pleased to be privy to it at last. It was difficult, in some ways, the Naughtiest Girl being a monitor.

As the noise level in the hall grew, Thomas had to bring the Meeting to order. He banged the gavel sharply on the small table.

'Silence! We're pleased you all like the idea! But if you've any questions or suggestions to make, please address them to the whole Meeting and not just to each other!'

Arabella was the first to put her hand up. She rose to her feet.

'Please, Thomas, Emma says we're allowed to put forward names for the award. But when should we do it exactly?'

'At any time, Arabella. At any time you see someone in your own form behaving in a way that deserves a nomination. The school office has a supply of special forms, called citation forms. You simply collect a form, fill in the person's name and your reason for naming them, then hand it to your monitor.'

'What happens to the forms then?' asked Arabella, eagerly.

'Any monitor who has been given a citation form will read it out, at the next Monitors' Meeting. Each one will be heard out in the privacy of that meeting. The best will go on a shortlist. Just before half-term, Emma and I will go through the shortlist with Miss Belle and Miss Best. They will help us to decide who has won the first William and Rita Award. But the Award will be presented once every term. It will, we hope, become a regular feature of school life and something that all can strive for.'

'Thank you, Thomas,' nodded Arabella. She sat down, her dainty face a little pinker than usual.

There were a few more questions. After that, the Meeting was declared closed.

Patrick waited for Elizabeth as she came out of the hall and pulled her to one side. He seemed agitated.

'I couldn't bear it, Elizabeth. You do understand, don't you? You do promise?'

'Of course I promise, Patrick.'

She patted his arm soothingly and smiled. She was feeling in a very good mood. How well the announcement had gone. The whole school approved of it! Thomas and Emma were absolutely right; courage and kindness and unselfishness were the most important qualities in the world. It was right that they should be recognized.

'You are much too modest, Patrick,' she said. 'But your secret is safe with me. I can't help wishing you would change your mind, though! You were so brave!'

At that moment, Julian came out of the hall, looking for Elizabeth. He was confronted by the sight of her with Patrick. The pair of them were whispering together, smiling and looking at each other in a silly way.

'Come on, Elizabeth,' he said sharply. 'Let's go and have tea.'

'Just coming, Julian!'

As they made their way to the dining-hall together, a feeling of exasperation swept over Julian.

'You seem to be getting very thick with my horrible cousin,' he commented.

'Oh, please don't be silly, Julian,' replied Elizabeth.

She was thinking hard. The glimmering of an idea was forming in her mind. She had thought of a way in which she could recognize Patrick's modesty and courage with a small noble deed of her own. It was no more than he deserved and it would be a gesture that she would find deeply satisfying.

Unfortunately, it was going to annoy Julian even more.

'Drat! I've got a horrid headache,' announced Elizabeth the next day. 'I don't think I'm going to be well enough to play in my match today!'

Julian stared at his friend in surprise.

It was Saturday dinner-time. Elizabeth had been laughing and talking cheerfully during the meal and had eaten heartily. The boys and girls had been out blackberrying during the week. From the bags full of succulent fruit brought to the school kitchens, Cook had concocted a whole shelf-full of summer puddings. They had been served today, with a choice of cream or custard. Elizabeth had eaten three helpings. Delicious!

'You must have eaten too much,' observed Julian.

'Oh, poor Elizabeth,' said Joan anxiously. 'But you mustn't miss the match! The coach leaves in twenty minutes ... You'd better go and see Matron for some aspirin straight away!'

Further along the table, Patrick's ears had pricked up.

'It's no good, Joan!' Elizabeth ran her hand across her brow for dramatic effect. 'I just know I won't be able to play my best today. Patrick will have to play in my place. He's first reserve and he is very good, you know.'

For a moment, Patrick had felt upset that

Elizabeth was feeling unwell. But now, unable to help himself, a look of incredulous joy crossed his face. The Naughtiest Girl felt very pleased with herself as she noted his expression.

'Oh, Elizabeth, I'll be glad to take your place if you're not feeling up to it. Shall we go and see Emma right away and talk to her about it?'

'Yes, Patrick. Let's!'

They rushed off to see Emma, who was just leaving the seniors' table. It was almost time to go and get ready. As team captain, she agreed at once that Patrick should take Elizabeth's place. A jolting coach journey to Hickling Green School would make the headache much worse for Elizabeth, she reasoned.

As Patrick and Elizabeth walked back to their own table, Julian strained his ears to hear what was being said. Elizabeth was gazing at Patrick with that silly expression on her face again. Patrick was talking to her as though they were very dear friends.

'Oh, Elizabeth, I've been waiting for this chance for so long. I won't let you down,

I promise. I'll play the best table tennis of my life.'

'I know you will, Patrick.'

'And I'll do it specially for you, Elizabeth! I'm going to win my match today, as a present for you.'

'Thank you, Patrick.'

'I don't think I've got time to finish my pudding. I'd better dash straight off and get changed and find my lucky table-tennis bat.'

He rushed away, brimming over with excitement. Elizabeth slipped back into her seat between Julian and Joan, a satisfied little smile on her face.

'Poor Elizabeth,' repeated Joan, who was just getting up from the table. 'What a shame. Promise me you'll have a quiet lie-down this afternoon.'

'We'll want to go and wave the coach off first, won't we, Joan?' replied Elizabeth, eagerly. 'We can wave to them and wish them good luck!'

Secretly, the Naughtiest Girl wanted to see

Patrick's face again as he climbed on to the coach in his smart tracksuit. That happy look on his face made it all so worthwhile.

'I can't, Elizabeth,' Joan apologized. 'I've promised to go on an outing with Susan this afternoon. Look, she's waiting for me now.'

Sure enough, Joan's friend Susan, who had gone up into the third form this term, was signalling to her. Miss Thomas was taking a group to the indoor swimming pool in the town and Susan was a very keen swimmer. Thinking that Elizabeth would be away at her match, Joan had arranged to go too.

As she hurried off, Elizabeth turned to Julian.

He was bent over his pudding, a puzzled gleam in his green eyes. He was a very clever, bright boy. He was not easily tricked. He was convinced that Elizabeth was play-acting and did not have a headache at all. She was trying to give Patrick a chance in the table-tennis team, that was all!

He was used to never knowing what went on inside her head. At other times, it was one of the things he liked best about her! But not today. Why was Elizabeth being so nice to his worthless cousin? It didn't make sense.

And Julian found it intensely irritating.

'You'll come with me to see Patrick off on the coach, won't you, Julian?' smiled Elizabeth. 'And it's a lovely afternoon. We could go out on the ponies, after that. We could have a good long outing.'

'Certainly not,' said Julian. 'Why should I want to see Patrick off on the coach? As for going for a ride, I thought you had a headache.'

'Well, yes, but . . .' Elizabeth thought quickly. 'I'm sure the fresh air will do it good!'

'I'm sorry, Elizabeth. I've fixed up to go riding with Harry and Robert. As you're not well enough to play in your match, I suggest you go and have a good lie-down, as Joan suggested.'

'Yes, of course,' sighed Elizabeth.

Soon after that she left the dining-hall and went outside into the school grounds, for a walk. She wanted to collect her thoughts. Julian was annoyed with her! He couldn't understand why she was being so friendly towards Patrick. If only she could explain to him what a fine person Patrick really was and that he *deserved* some reward. But she couldn't. She'd promised!

The coach was waiting on the back drive.

Shortly before it was due to leave, she went across there and hid in the shrubbery. She could see all the boys and girls climbing aboard, the hockey team as well. They were all laughing and talking together. Patrick was already in his seat, on the far side of the coach, so she couldn't see his expression, after all. Unable to wave the coach off with her friends, she knew she would feel a bit silly doing it on her own. So she decided to watch it leave, from here, without being seen.

The warm glow that she'd felt a few minutes earlier had faded. As she watched the last passengers climb aboard and the coach doors shut, she felt very wistful. They were all off to Hickling Green without her. She was going to miss all the excitement! And what was she going to do with herself? The afternoon stretched ahead, bleak and empty . . .

As the coach moved away and trundled off down the drive, a figure standing behind it was suddenly revealed. He was waving, rather forlornly.

It was Jake, seeing the coach off.

But as soon as the vehicle disappeared, Jake's arm dropped to his side and he did an extraordinary thing.

Never dreaming that Elizabeth was watching him from her hiding place, Jake shook his fist at the sky then ran furiously down the drive after the coach and took a flying kick at some loose gravel, to relieve his feelings. He then ran off down a side path and disappeared from view.

'He was running!' realized Elizabeth. 'He didn't have a limp at all! He must have been pretending all this time. There's nothing wrong with his ankle whatsoever!'

It was a very surprising discovery.

5   *Elizabeth gives Jake away*

Elizabeth followed in Jake's tracks.

'He's limping again, now that people can see him!' she realized, as she reached the other end of the path where it emerged from the bushes. Here, some junior boys and girls were playing on the back lawn.

Jake limped slowly past them, heading for the school buildings. For a moment she wondered if she could have just dreamt it. But only for a moment.

'No. I definitely saw what I saw. So why is Jake play-acting like this?' thought Elizabeth, hot-temperedly. 'It's so mean of him! How can he bear to let our form down in this way, as well as the hockey team and the whole of Whyteleafe School!'

She very nearly dashed after him, there and

then. But, even with her temper up, she did not quite dare to confront him. Besides, he was surrounded by some junior boys now. Jake was one of their heroes.

What should she do?

'Julian will know the best thing to do!' Elizabeth decided. 'I'll ask his advice. I'd better run all the way, if I want to catch him before he goes off!'

She raced across the grounds to the school stables. But the boys had just left.

'They went that way, Elizabeth,' the stableman told her, pointing up the bridle path.

'Thanks!' gasped Elizabeth.

She veered off through the trees. She could hear voices some distance ahead and the clip-clop of the ponies' hooves. Then, through a gap, she glimpsed them turning off at right angles, where the path divided. They were riding in single file, Robert, then Harry, Julian bringing up the rear. She scrambled over a bank and through tangled undergrowth, to cut off a corner. It brought her within hailing distance.

She cupped her hands to her mouth.

'JULIAN!' she shouted, with all her might.

Startled, Julian reined in his pony. He wheeled the animal round and spotted Elizabeth, frantically waving her arms. He told Harry and Robert to wait for him.

He trotted back to meet her.

'Whatever's wrong, Elizabeth?'

Gulping to get her breath back, she told Julian what she had just discovered. She was bristling with indignation. He listened carefully.

Then, to her surprise, he gave a dry laugh.

'So that's two of you trying to get out of playing in school matches, is it?' he commented. 'You're a fine one to be cross, Elizabeth. How's the headache, by the way?'

Elizabeth fell silent.

Julian spoke more gently then.

'I think you must have imagined it about Jake, you know.'

'I did not, Julian. I certainly did not! I was hoping to hear your ideas – about the best thing to do.'

'Well, I know that *you* have a reason for getting out of *your* match, Elizabeth. Even if it is a totally potty one! So *Jake* may have a reason, too. You will have to go and speak to him and ask him to explain. After all . . .'

Down the bridle path, Harry and Robert were signalling impatiently. They were cross to have been held up like this. Julian wheeled his pony round. He was suddenly feeling rather cross himself.

'. . . *You* are the monitor, Elizabeth, not me. Good luck!'

Julian rode off then, without a backward glance. He was annoyed to have been reminded like this of Elizabeth making sacrifices on behalf of his worthless cousin, Patrick. Just when he had managed to put it out of his mind!

Elizabeth walked slowly back to school, feeling very subdued.

Her temper had evaporated now. Julian's words had rather shamed her. He had guessed that she had made it up about the headache. He had also guessed the reason why! She longed to explain to him about Patrick's brave deed but she was not allowed to. And, of course, Julian was right. She was a fine one to feel indignant about Jake!

But she also knew that Julian's advice was correct. As Jake's monitor, she should go and speak to him and give him a chance to explain the reason for his strange behaviour. She should then persuade Jake to go and own up to the teachers. However, Elizabeth remembered the last time that she had spoken to the big boy as his monitor. How grumpy he had been with her – and with good reason, with so much to hide.

How much grumpier he would be if she dared to confront him now! And he would probably think that she had been spying on him. He would be furious!

All that afternoon, Elizabeth tried to screw up courage to go and speak to the older boy. But her courage failed her. She decided that perhaps she would speak to Joan about it, at teatime. If Joan agreed, they would go and see Jake together, this evening.

It was only when Joan did not turn up at teatime that Elizabeth remembered that the swimming group had been excused tea today. They were having tea in town.

Julian turned up late, glowing from his ride, and did not even bother to ask Elizabeth if she had spoken to Jake yet. Elizabeth was relieved about that.

After that, she did her piano practice and then decided to go and wait for the return of the school coach. She longed to know how the table-tennis team had got on at Hickling Green. What fun Patrick would have been having today, so much more fun than her. She'd never known such a dreary time. How she would have loved to play in the match!

The first person off the coach was Mr Warlow.

'Hello, Elizabeth. Feeling better? You'll be pleased to know that we won the table tennis. Patrick played very well.'

Elizabeth felt some relief at those words. She

had done the school no harm then, by not playing in the match! But – she had never seen the sports master look so careworn.

'Is there anything wrong, Mr Warlow?' she asked.

'I'm afraid the hockey match was a disaster. We were beaten 6–0. We had our chances to score but we didn't take them. We needed our star shooter and that's a fact. It would have made such a difference if Jake had played. That wretched ankle of his. I have never known a simple sprain take so long to get better!'

The young sports master looked so unhappy, Elizabeth longed to cheer him up! She smiled impetuously and, before she could stop them, the words flew out of her mouth, unbidden.

'It's better now, Mr Warlow! It's just got better!'

'Elizabeth, is this true?' asked the teacher, looking excited. 'Have you spoken to Jake, then?'

Elizabeth gulped. What had she said? What had she *done*?

There was no going back now.

'I – I haven't actually spoken to him. But I saw him outside and the ankle's suddenly looking . . . well, really fine. I'm sure it's going to be all right for the match against Milford Grange, Mr Warlow! I'm sure if you get Jake to have a check-up . . .'

'I'll drive him to the doctor myself!' exclaimed Mr Warlow, in delight. 'I'll go and find him straight away! If we hurry, we'll just make surgery before it closes.'

He strode briskly away.

'This is very good news, Elizabeth!' he called back over his shoulder. 'Thank you so much for telling me! What a good monitor you are!'

'Hello, Elizabeth! What's this about good news? I've got some good news myself!'

Patrick had appeared at her side. Some members of the Whyteleafe first hockey team were beginning to trudge past, heads bowed, eyes downcast. But Patrick was beaming with pride.

'I won both my games, Elizabeth!' he was

saying. 'I told you I would, didn't I?'

Elizabeth was watching Mr Warlow, as he disappeared into the school building. He was determined to find Jake at once. He wanted to take him to the doctor's! What a shock the big boy was going to get. Elizabeth could not help feeling a little trembly. She had let her tongue run away with her.

With an effort, she turned her attention to Patrick.

'Congratulations!' she said, looking pale. 'I'm so pleased for you. Was it a good outing then?'

'A marvellous outing! We had the most splendid tea!' Patrick was looking elated. 'But you haven't heard the half of it, Elizabeth! Donald didn't play at all well today. If it hadn't been for me, we'd have lost. My last game decided it. From something Emma said to me, I think I'm going to be chosen instead of Donald next time.'

They started to walk over to the school together.

'Oh, Patrick, I'm so glad I gave you your chance!' Elizabeth blurted out. 'It's no more than you deserve.'

'Gave me my chance?' asked Patrick, looking puzzled.

Elizabeth took a deep breath. She had been stung by Julian's words earlier. It would make her feel better if Patrick, at least, knew the truth . . .

'I didn't really have a headache,' she confessed. 'I was just desperate to make sure that you got some reward at least for your brave deed.'

'Elizabeth!' exclaimed Patrick. He looked horrified. 'You shouldn't have done that.'

'I had to,' she replied. 'You are such a fine person, Patrick. I don't know how I'm going to hold my tongue at the next MM, I really don't . . . you do deserve the William and Rita Award, you really do!'

'No!' The boy paled. 'You promised!'

'It's all right, it's all right,' she said soothingly. Seeing how upset he was, she slipped her arm through his as they walked towards the school steps together. 'Only joking, Patrick! I am sure a lot of fine deeds will be coming up at the MMs. I expect Thomas and Emma will have far too many to choose from when the time comes! I must say I'm looking forward to hearing some of them.'

Patrick nodded, visibly relieved. He liked having Elizabeth on his arm like this. Somebody was coming down the steps, and would be passing right by them in a moment . . .

'Hello, Julian!' he said cheerfully. 'I won my games today! Nice evening, isn't it?'

'Is it?' asked Julian, curtly. 'Joan's back, Elizabeth. She was looking for you.'

And he passed on his way.

Elizabeth took her leave of Patrick almost immediately.

She found Joan resting on the bed upstairs.

'Oh, Elizabeth, I have had such a wonderful time! But I am quite exhausted now!'

Gentle Joan had never shone at sports. But

today she had made an exciting discovery. It seemed that Miss Thomas believed that she had the talents of a born swimmer. The teacher was hoping to get up a Whyteleafe swimming team some time. She had told Joan that, with the right training, she could well be a member of it.

'Miss Thomas is going to give Susan and me and some others regular fitness training in the gym,' Joan explained. 'Oh, Elizabeth, I never thought I'd ever be good at sports but I really think I might enjoy swimming.'

'Joan, this is the most thrilling news!' exclaimed Elizabeth, pleased to see her friend so happy.

For once Joan was too full of her own news to question her friend about the headache, or how she'd spent the afternoon. That came as a relief to Elizabeth.

She was beginning to feel very ashamed that instead of having the courage to go and speak to Jake, she had ended up blurting out his secret to a teacher. She could not bring herself to confess what she had done, even to her best friend.

But what would happen now?

6 A horrid message appears

On Sunday morning, Jake was seen running up and down the hockey pitch with Mr Warlow, practising his stick work. The teacher wanted to see his star player back on top form as quickly as possible. He would be needed for the Milford Grange match, needed very badly!

Several second form boys turned out to watch him. Martin, Kenneth, Harry and John McTavish were all fans of his. He was such a marvellous player for a boy of his age; Kenneth was already a friend of his in the second form. The others had admired him even when they were only in the first form.

It was great news, the boys all agreed, that the sprained ankle had now made a complete recovery. Mr Warlow had got the doctor to check it over last night. There had been no sign of bruise or swelling there. He was pronounced fit to play hockey again.

'What a shame it wasn't in time to play against Hickling Green yesterday!' observed Harry.

'But he'll be able to play against Milford Grange!' smiled Martin. 'It's a home match so we'll all be able to watch!'

'We'll thrash them!' said John jubilantly. 'Jake will see to that.'

They were all very pleased.

'Did you speak to Jake then, Elizabeth?' asked Julian, with interest, at one point during the day.

'Not exactly,' she mumbled, in embarrassment, and hurried off.

For the only person who was not pleased was Jake.

Secretly, he was very upset. He did not want to play hockey against Milford Grange. He did not want to play hockey at all. When he passed Elizabeth in the dining-hall at breakfast-time, he had given her such a fierce look. Mr Warlow might think that Elizabeth was a good monitor, to have spotted that Jake's ankle had suddenly made a recovery, but Jake did not share that opinion! He was very taken aback by it all and became convinced that Elizabeth must have been spying on him, in secret. How long had she been doing so? he wondered.

She had also got him into trouble. For the doctor had informed Mr Warlow that from all appearances any injury to the ankle must have repaired itself some time ago. The teacher was baffled that Jake had made out the injury to be far worse than it really was. He had accused him of laziness and of letting down the school.

Jake was such a big, silent, powerful character. The fierce look he had given Elizabeth had made her flinch! She spent the rest of the day avoiding him. She was very puzzled by his strange behaviour. At the same time she was truly ashamed that his secret had come out in the way that it had. She wanted to find some way of showing him that she was sorry.

By the evening, when she felt hopeful that Jake would have cooled down somewhat, she took her chance. He was standing drinking cocoa in the second form common room, surrounded by the gang of boys who admired him.

'Have my chocolate biscuit, Jake,' she said, walking up to him. 'It will build you up for the match against Milford Grange! May I come and cheer you on, please?'

'Don't bother,' replied Jake curtly, ignoring the plate. 'I can manage without you.'

Elizabeth had a hot temper. It immediately flared up.

'How rude!' she gasped, gazing up at the boy as he towered above her. 'You're not to talk to a monitor like that!'

That immediately inflamed Jake.

'I'm tired of girl monitors,' he stated. 'Little girl monitors would do a lot better to mind their own business.'

'Hear, hear!' agreed Martin. He had no idea what Jake was talking about but he could see that the big boy was very angry.

Elizabeth's own anger easily matched Jake's.

She wanted to blurt out that it was not just her business but everybody else's if a person pretended they had something wrong with them when they hadn't and deliberately let a school team down! But then, to her horror, she remembered that she'd just done the same thing herself. Even if, by good fortune, Patrick had won his games and prevented the table-tennis team from being defeated.

She bit back her words, turned on her heel and marched out of the common room.

She slammed the door loudly behind her.

'What's up between you and her, Jake?' asked his friend Kenneth.

'She told tales, that's all,' replied Jake, looking morose. 'She exceeded her authority. She shouldn't poke her nose in my private business. I'm fed up with bossy girl monitors thinking they know what's best for us boys.'

'Joan doesn't do that,' Harry pointed out, fairly.

'No,' agreed Martin. 'And she's been one for ages. Elizabeth's new, which makes it worse.'

'I expect it's gone right to her curly head,' sighed Jake, wearily.

He clammed up then. He became his usual strong, silent self and refused to answer any more questions.

But after he'd left the common room, the other boys were all agog.

They liked the Naughtiest Girl. But they all knew how she'd got her nickname! And there was no doubt that she could still be headstrong and impulsive and do crazy things sometimes. They admired Jake and they trusted him. If he was angry with Elizabeth then she must have seriously overstepped the mark in some way.

'She wanted to wear a monitor's armband, didn't she, Harry?' remembered Martin. 'And Julian teased her and said it would make her look like a member of the secret police!'

'And it sounds as though she's been behaving

like one!' commented John McTavish. 'What a nerve, telling tales on someone like Jake. Thinking she knows what's best for him.'

'I wonder what it was all about?' pondered Harry.

The news of the quarrel spread around the boys' dormitories that night, and grew in the telling. The joke about the armband, and the secret police, was also passed around.

Julian felt rather badly when he heard his joke being repeated. He was going to say something in Elizabeth's defence but then Patrick stepped in.

'Elizabeth is a very good sort!' he declared. 'Shut up, all of you.'

So Julian shrugged his shoulders and said nothing.

Elizabeth slept badly that night. There were tears of frustration in her eyes. She so much wanted to be a successful monitor but things were starting to go wrong.

At breakfast-time, on Monday morning, she

could tell that some of the boys had started to turn against her.

'Where's your armband, Elizabeth?' Martin teased her. 'We won't know to do what we're told if you don't wear an armband.'

Arabella tittered loudly.

'It's not that funny, Arabella,' said Julian, airily. 'It's rather an old joke by now. Can't you think of a new one, Martin?'

Elizabeth was glad to escape from the dining-hall.

She went up to Room 14 to clean her shoes and brush her hair and get ready for lessons. Joan, Kathleen and Jenny, who had all been sitting at the other table today, drifted in. Elizabeth enjoyed chatting about other things with her room-mates and began to feel a bit better.

Drat boys! she thought. It was fun just being with girls sometimes! She began to look forward to her first lesson, which was French, with Mam'zelle.

'Let's get down to the form room nice and early,' suggested Joan.

'Yes!' nodded Elizabeth. 'My desk needs a bit of a tidy-up.'

The form room was empty when they arrived. The two friends had adjoining desks. Elizabeth boisterously flung up her desk lid.

'Oh!'

She quickly closed it again, her cheeks pale.

'What was that?' asked Joan quickly. 'What was that piece of paper taped to the inside of your desk lid?'

'It – it seems to be some kind of horrid message,' said Elizabeth.

Gently, Joan opened the desk lid again.

Together, the two friends gazed in silence at the anonymous message, carefully written in block capitals.

WHY HAS THE SECOND FORM GOT TWO GIRL MONITORS? NOT FAIR! GIVE DANIEL HIS CHANCE BACK, ELIZABETH. GIVE THE BOYS A MONITOR OF THEIR OWN!

*   *   *

At that moment Mr Leslie, their form-master, came into the classroom to put some things away. Joan carefully removed the message, folded it and placed it in her pocket. They would have to discuss it later.

7 *Things go from bad to worse*

'What's all this about, Elizabeth?' asked Joan, at morning break. 'Have you any idea who could have written it?'

'I believe I know exactly who has written it!' replied Elizabeth.

The two friends were sitting on the school steps in the pale October sunshine. Joan had taken the piece of paper from her pocket and unfolded it. Why had somebody turned against Elizabeth? It was all very upsetting.

'Who?' asked Joan, in surprise.

'Jake, of course!' Elizabeth blurted out. 'How mean of him not to sign it. What an underhand thing to do!'

'*Jake?*' asked Joan. She liked the gentle giant of a boy and felt she knew him quite well. He had joined the second form even earlier than she had. 'Why ever should Jake be feeling cross with you, Elizabeth? Especially as I'm sure he must be in a very good mood at the moment with his poor ankle better.'

'That's just it, Joan! He's not in a good mood at all about his ankle! He should be, but he isn't. And he's simply furious with me!'

Joan's eyes widened. She spoke gently.

'What's been going on, Elizabeth? What have you been keeping from me?'

Shamefaced, Elizabeth told Joan everything that had happened concerning Jake the previous day. It was a relief to do so, at last.

But Joan, as Elizabeth feared she would be, was very disapproving.

'It was very wrong of you to speak to Mr Warlow before you had spoken to Jake himself, Elizabeth!' she scolded. 'You know that's not the way we do things at Whyteleafe. Jake must have had some very private reason of his own for wanting to get out of hockey, something that he was determined to keep secret. As his monitor, you should have asked him to talk it through with you and then tried to persuade him to go and own up to Mr Warlow. No wonder he is cross with you!'

'I was too scared to,' Elizabeth confessed. 'I was sure Jake didn't respect me as a monitor and the note proves I was right. He thinks the other monitor should be a boy! And because I've upset Jake, some more of the boys are turning against me! What should I do, Joan? Do you think I should resign?'

'Of course not, Elizabeth!' her friend replied, firmly. She folded the note up and replaced it in her pocket. 'You can't give in to this sort of thing. It's not always easy being a monitor and we all make mistakes. Just try to tread carefully for a while, Elizabeth. Everybody likes you very much and wanted you to be a monitor this term. I'm sure this will all blow over in a few days.'

'Oh, do you really think so, Joan?'

Elizabeth felt very cheered.

But her cheerfulness did not last long.

Far from blowing over, the trouble with the boys got worse.

Elizabeth was still being teased. And the feeling that it was unfair not to have a boy monitor seemed to be spreading. Jake continued to be unfriendly towards her and Elizabeth strongly suspected that, as well as writing the note, he was encouraging the other boys in some kind of campaign to get rid of her. Had she made a powerful enemy?

In Martin's dormitory, they were starting to have pillow fights at night. These were forbidden, of course, but apparently great fun!

Martin openly bragged that, as girls were not allowed to enter the boys' quarters, they could do what they liked as they only had girl monitors in the second form. No monitors could come and stop their fun!

Julian gave Elizabeth a friendly word of warning.

'I shouldn't report them, if I were you, Elizabeth,' he said. 'Not if you know what's good for you!'

Elizabeth had never actually admitted to Julian that she'd given Jake's secret away because she and Julian were far less close than usual. She was sad but there was nothing she could do about it, without explaining to him the story of Patrick's bravery. However, on the Jake front, Julian had very quickly worked things out for himself. Like Elizabeth, he was mystified as to why the big boy had pretended about the injury in the first place.

'Don't worry, Julian,' she sighed. 'I know I'm in enough trouble already. I haven't the slightest intention of reporting them.'

She would love to have had a proper chat with him about everything. But he was already strolling away, whistling.

Patrick was a real nuisance! she thought.

She thought so again, the following day.

The next Monitors' Meeting was due. In Elizabeth's class, only one written nomination had been handed in. Quivering with importance, Rosemary had handed the special form over to Joan. But Joan was not able to attend this week's MM. Miss Thomas had arranged the first fitness session for the would-be swimming team. It would clash directly with the MM but it was the teacher's only free time. Joan dare not miss her very first workout.

'I'm afraid that you are going to have to read this out at the MM, Elizabeth,' she said later, with a wry smile, passing across Rosemary's form. 'What a lovely job for you!'

'Oh, no!' groaned Elizabeth, reading what was written there. 'This is going to be so embarrassing. Must I really? Ugh!'

They both laughed.

Nevertheless, after lessons that day, Elizabeth set off eagerly for the MM. This was going to be very interesting. What kind of citations would the other monitors be reading out, from their classmates? Surely they'd be more exciting than Rosemary's? She certainly hoped so!

She arrived on time this week and collected her mug of tea. There were chocolate digestive biscuits again. Good!

'It's all right, Elizabeth, there are plenty. You

may take two!' smiled Emma.

She settled down on the floor, next to Peter, letting Donald have the place on the bench. It was quite comfortable on the floor this week as Thomas had managed to find some cushions.

'Hello, Peter,' she said to the young first form monitor. 'Have you been given any citations yet for the William and Rita Award?'

Peter shook his head. He seemed to have something else on his mind.

'Not yet, Elizabeth. I keep asking for them, though.'

Soon all the monitors had crammed into the cosy study. Elizabeth was disappointed to see that not many had brought citations with them. She gave Joan's apologies. Then various minor school matters were discussed. Peter put his hand up.

'Please, Thomas and Emma, can you all give me some advice? Some of the boys in my class were squirting water pistols indoors. They wouldn't stop when I asked, so I confiscated them. When d'you think I should give them back?'

They all discussed Peter's problem.

'There we are, then! We're all agreed,' Thomas concluded. 'You can keep them for a week. A week seems quite a long time when you're in the first form! Then, as long as they promise only to play with them out of doors in future, you can hand them back!'

At last it was time for the citations to be read out.

'You first, Elizabeth,' said Emma. 'I can see you've got one in your hand.'

'It's only just the one so far, I'm afraid,' apologized Elizabeth. 'It's been submitted by Rosemary Wing.'

She tried her best to hide her embarrassment as she read out loud the second form's only citation.

Yesterday, my hamster looked very droopy and I was worried about him. Then Arabella Buckley performed a very unselfish act. Arabella is very fond of chocolate herself but she sacrificed all the chocolate she had left for the whole week and fed it to Hammy, so as to cheer him up. I would therefore like to nominate Arabella Buckley for the William and Rita Award.

Some of the monitors snorted and sniggered.

'I expect poor Hammy was sick on the spot!' whispered Donald.

Elizabeth's cheeks burned. She felt so ashamed of her classmates. It was obvious that Arabella had put Rosemary up to this! Surely, between them, they could at least have invented something better? She'd tried her best to read it nicely and put the correct expression in her voice. But it had still sounded completely silly.

'Thank you, Elizabeth,' said Emma, sympathetically. 'That was very nicely read.'

'And those of you who are giggling, I'm ashamed of you,' added Thomas. 'All citations are to be listened to in silence, please. I think we are all agreed that this one's not suitable for the shortlist, so let us pass on.'

Elizabeth at once felt better. Now that the

second form citation had been dealt with, she could settle down and look forward to hearing the other forms' contributions.

But there were, indeed, only a few. And although they were all much more genuine than Rosemary's effort, they were not very inspiring.

After hearing out the last one, read by Eric, the head boy and girl shook their heads.

'I don't think anything we have heard today is quite suitable for the shortlist, do you?' asked Emma, ruefully. 'The William and Rita Award must be given for an act of real courage or unselfishness, not everyday acts of kindness, pleasing though it is to hear about them.'

'We seem to have got off to a slow start, I'm afraid,' agreed Thomas. 'Luckily there's plenty of time yet. We must look forward to something really splendid coming in over the next couple of weeks.'

But Elizabeth could tell that they were both very disappointed.

It was so frustrating! How she longed to tell them that a member of the second form *had* performed an act of real courage.

As she left the MM, she decided that she must go and find Patrick at once. He had just finished a game of table tennis with Daniel.

'Listen, Patrick, I've been thinking,' she said, as she took him outside. There was a pleading note in her voice. 'You know, about your brave deed. I know you don't want it talked about and I know you must be worried that you broke a school rule that day, being down in the village on your own. But supposing, when I go to the next MM, I just talk about this certain boy, without giving his name away? Supposing I just talk about this certain boy being worried about breaking this strict rule and see if they think that matters . . . ? And then . . .'

'Elizabeth! Stop being so tiresome!' exclaimed Patrick, impatiently. 'I am not in the least bit worried about being punished for breaking a school rule. That has nothing to do with it really!'

'But . . .'

'I just don't want to be held up as some kind

of hero, Elizabeth!' He stared at her, looking baffled and angry. 'Why are you bringing all this up again?'

'I'm sorry, Patrick. I just wondered if perhaps – well, all us monitors want the first William and Rita Award to be something really special! Can't you see that? And I thought, if it was just the school rule you were worried about . . .'

'Well, it's not!' Patrick almost shouted the words. 'Please forget the whole thing. You promised.'

'I – I'll try.'

'Drop it, Elizabeth! Please don't mention this again!'

Elizabeth walked away after that.

She was still filled with admiration for Patrick. How could she not be? But it was very annoying of him, all the same. The William and Rita Award was such a lovely idea. But supposing nobody came forward with anything worthwhile by half-term? Thomas and Emma would not be able to make the award, after all. What a bad start that would be.

Nothing seemed to be going right at the moment.

In fact things went from bad to worse.

When she went along to collect some homework from her desk, after tea, there was another anonymous message stuck inside the lid. Once again, it was written in block capitals:

SOME OF US ARE FED UP. THERE ARE PILLOW FIGHTS NOW – KEEPING US AWAKE AT NIGHT. THE SECOND FORM NEEDS A BOY MONITOR TO KEEP ORDER. WHY NOT RESIGN PLEASE, ELIZABETH?

Paling slightly, she hurried outside to find Joan.

8 The Naughtiest Girl versus the boys

'My so-called secret enemy has struck again, Joan!' she said crossly, showing Joan the message. 'Not all that secret, in fact. I'm quite convinced that it's Jake who's writing these notes. I know I'm a coward, Joan, but shall we go and see him together and tell him to stop it? He might take some notice of you.'

'We can't do that, Elizabeth,' replied Joan, biting her lip as she read the note carefully. 'We can't be sure it's Jake. Is this really Jake's sort of thing? And we certainly can't walk up to him and accuse him without any proof!'

'I suppose not,' sighed Elizabeth. She read the note through carefully, once again. 'To be fair, it must be very annoying for Jake if these pillow fights are keeping him awake.'

'If it is Jake,' Joan reminded her, gently.

'Well, Jake or whoever it is. Anybody who doesn't specially enjoy pillow fights,' said Elizabeth. She was looking thoughtful. 'As I *am* a monitor, I should be thinking what to do.'

'I shouldn't worry, Elizabeth!' said Joan hastily, noting the light in her eye. 'We can't take any notice of anonymous messages. If anyone comes forward with a proper complaint about losing a lot of sleep, then that would be serious and you'd have to report it to the teachers.'

'What, tell tales?' asked Elizabeth, aghast, remembering Julian's advice to her. 'But that would make my position even worse, Joan.'

'This would be quite different, Elizabeth. You couldn't possibly deal with a whole crowd of boys on your own. But, of course, someone would have to make a formal complaint first, not just write a silly note like this. And I don't suppose anybody will.'

Elizabeth did not follow Joan's logic. In

any case, she was hardly listening.

She'd suddenly remembered young Peter's water pistols and an excited gleam came into her eye. She knew exactly how to handle this problem! She certainly didn't want anybody making a formal complaint to either Joan or herself and then having to go to the teachers. She didn't agree with Joan at all about that. The boys would never forgive them.

She must act quickly, before there was any danger of it happening.

Later, a cheerful sparkle in her eye, Elizabeth slipped off to talk to some of the other girls. They were good sports, all of them.

Then she went to find Peter.

'I'm not going to involve Joan in this,' she thought. 'But I'll jolly well show those boys who's the monitor around here!'

Even as Elizabeth was borrowing the water pistols from Peter, an even younger boy was seeking out Joan, for the junior class did not have a monitor of its own. The small boy was in pyjamas and dressing-gown but was not looking forward to going to bed. For two nights running he'd been woken up by bumpings and crashings in the second form dormitory and had been unable to get to sleep again. His bed was right against the dividing wall. There were dark rings under his eyes.

'Go straight to bed now, Rupert,' Joan told him, after hearing him out. 'I'll see this is sorted out. I'll see to it myself, I promise.'

'And I won't involve Elizabeth,' she thought. It's true what she says. 'She is in enough trouble already.'

After that, Joan decided, she would go to bed herself. The fitness training in the gym had been very enjoyable but had left her tired out and aching in every muscle.

'Sssh, Kathleen! Sssh, Jenny!' whispered Elizabeth. 'We mustn't wake Joan!'

'No danger of that, Elizabeth. She's dead to the world!' Kathleen whispered back.

'Miss Thomas really puts them through it, I gather!' commented Jenny.

'Such luck!' giggled Kathleen.

'Sssh!' repeated Elizabeth.

It was after Lights Out, and the three girls had slipped out of bed and were putting on their dressing-gowns and slippers. They had waited until they were sure that Joan was in a very deep sleep. On no account, Elizabeth explained, did she want to involve Joan in her plan.

'I shall take full responsibility for this,' she had told her room-mates earlier. 'I don't want to have to report those boys to the teachers and I don't want Joan to either. They think it's so clever having pillow fights but we'll soon cool them down!'

Belinda and Tessa were waiting for them in the corridor.

'Got the water pistols, Elizabeth?' whispered Belinda, eagerly.

'I've hidden them in the bathroom!' the Naughtiest Girl whispered back.

The five girls tiptoed along the corridor to the big bathroom. They were all trying hard not to giggle. This was going to be such an adventure! Elizabeth took the five water pistols out from their hiding place in the big linen box.

She handed her friends one each.

'Right,' she said. 'Now let's load them. As full as full can be.'

With Elizabeth their commander-in-chief leading the way, the girls crept along the dimly lit corridors until they reached the boys' quarters. Their pistols were at the ready, loaded with water up to the hilt.

'Martin's dormitory,' she whispered crisply. 'Number 17. Just at the bottom of these stairs. Come on, now. Party – advance!'

'I think I can hear them now,' whispered Kathleen excitedly, as they crept down the short flight of stairs. 'Voices!'

The door was ajar. There seemed to be torches flashing around inside. It was after Lights Out but there were figures moving about and some whispering going on. The nightly pillow fight must be just about to commence!

Eyes sparkling with anticipation, Elizabeth waved her water pistol above her head in a signal to the other four.

'Ready, steady – CHARGE!' she hissed.

With their monitor at their head, the girls hurled themselves down the last few stairs and burst into Room 17.

'FIRE!' cried Elizabeth and they squeezed the triggers, spraying fine jets of water at the figures that moved in the dark.

'Break it up, boys!'

'Cool down!'

'Pillow fights not allowed!'

As they shouted their war cries, the girls were laughing with glee.

'Bulls-eye!' cried Elizabeth, as she squirted her best jet of water towards the back of somebody's neck.

'Got you!' she added triumphantly. 'Now perhaps *that* will cool you down just a little bit . . .'

At that very moment the figure turned, receiving it full in the face.

'ELIZABETH ALLEN!' roared the person, shining his torch on her. 'What on earth do you think you are doing?'

Elizabeth and her friends recoiled in dismay. It was a man's voice. They knew it well. Elizabeth shone her own torch, while behind her somebody switched on a light.

Elizabeth found herself face to face with Mr Leslie, their form-master. He had three senior boys with him, including Thomas, the head boy. These were the only figures who'd been moving around! They were holding torches. All of them had water dripping down their shirts. Martin and co., from all appearances, were asleep in bed. Only now were tousled heads raising themselves from various pillows.

'Hey!'

'What's going on?'

'Who's put that light on?'

– came the innocent-sounding cries.

Elizabeth stared at her teacher in horror.

'I'm t-t-terribly sorry, sir,' she stammered.

Mr Leslie looked very cross.

'And so you should be, Elizabeth. We were told there might be some horseplay tonight but we expected to find *boys* misbehaving not girls. Please return to your own quarters this instant, all of you.'

The five girls dived out of the door, in relief. They couldn't wait to escape! From the stairs, they heard Thomas's voice.

'It's all right, boys. Sorry you've been disturbed. You can go back to sleep now.'

The girls returned to their quarters in silence. What a disaster, thought Jenny and co. Somehow the boys had got wind of Elizabeth's plan and neatly turned the tables. When the girl monitor and her troops had turned up to put a stop to the boys' pillow fights, they'd run straight into their teacher and his inspection party, with the second form boys pretending to be fast asleep!

The boys had won. The girls were going to get into trouble and Elizabeth, as ringleader, would get into the biggest trouble of all!

But all Elizabeth could think about, as she tried to get back to sleep that night, was her enemy. *Somebody* had reported her plan to Mr Leslie. And she was sure she knew who. What a mean thing to do!

But the next morning, she got a shock.

'Of course it wasn't Jake!' exclaimed Joan, in horror, as she listened to Elizabeth's tale of woe. 'Oh, Elizabeth, what a dreadful mix-up. What a dreadful thing to happen! It was me!'

'*You*, Joan?' squealed Elizabeth, in surprise.

Her loud squeal brought Jenny and Kathleen running over.

In distress, Joan explained to her room-mates about little Rupert.

'The child was desperate about it. He turned to me for help, as a monitor. It left me with no choice but to go and report to Mr Leslie that Room 17 was being noisy at nights, though I didn't say anything about the pillow fights. I'm sorry I didn't tell you, Elizabeth. I didn't want to involve you.'

'I'm sorry I didn't tell you about *my* plan,'

said Elizabeth, very shamefaced. 'Oh, what a muddle!'

'Thank goodness it wasn't one of the boys, anyway,' said Kathleen, with a sigh of relief.

'Yes, that makes us feel a bit better about it,' agreed Elizabeth. She frowned. 'But, Joan, how did Martin and co. know to be well-behaved last night? That's what I can't understand.'

Joan thought about it carefully.

'John McTavish walked past last night, when Rupert was talking to me in the corridor. I didn't think he had heard anything. But obviously he must have done.'

'Ah!' said Elizabeth.

So that, too, was explained.

When Mr Leslie came into class to take the register that morning, the boys owned up about the pillow fights. That, at least, came as a great relief to Elizabeth, Joan and co. They were a nice crowd really.

'Humph, yes, well I'm not stupid, Martin,' said Mr Leslie. 'I did realize that something must have been going on. That the fault would not be all on one side. As your high jinks have been depriving some of the other boys of their sleep, Thomas is going to raise the matter at this week's Meeting.'

'Is he going to raise the matter of Elizabeth, as well?' asked Jake, with interest. 'Our *monitor*.'

Some of the boys laughed.

Elizabeth flushed deeply at Jake's intervention.

'I understand that Elizabeth will be dealt with at the next Monitors' Meeting,' replied Mr Leslie, curtly. 'Now, will everybody please get their pencils and paper ready. Miss Ranger will be here very shortly and today's the day you have your spelling tests.'

After that Julian made some sympathetic 'hen clucking' noises to try to cheer Elizabeth up. He had heard all about the episode in Room 17 and had found it highly diverting. Would the Naughtiest Girl even last till half-term as a monitor? he wondered.

But Elizabeth was not amused. She concentrated hard on the weekly spelling test. After that, for the rest of the English lesson, she kept her head bent over her work. She felt a sense of despair. She had so much wanted to be a successful and popular monitor this term, one who enjoyed the respect of the whole form, like Joan. But she could see that Jake was not going to allow that to happen.

Of course, the water pistols had not been such a good idea. She had been silly and hot-headed and she could not blame Jake for that. But it was getting those horrid notes that had stirred her up and made her behave foolishly. Now some of the boys were laughing at her.

She smouldered as she thought of the notes and she came to a decision.

'I have decided to tackle Jake about those mean notes,' she whispered to Joan, toward the end of the lesson. 'I know you don't want to, so I've decided to speak to him on my own. I shall tell him what I think of him!'

Joan just looked helpless and shook her head.

At that moment Miss Ranger called the two monitors out.

'Elizabeth and Joan, would you please give everybody their spellings back? I have marked them now.'

As the two friends shared out the bundle between them, the English teacher spoke pleasantly to the class.

'Elizabeth and Joan will bring your spellings round. Julian has come top today with 20 out of 20. Jake, you would have had full marks, but once again you forgot your silent Gs. You always forget them! You spelt both SIGN and RESIGN without the G! When you think of SIGN, think of SIGNATURE and that will help you remember. And when you spell RESIGN, think of RESIGNATION. It's a shame you have such a blank spot about this, or you would have come equal top . . .'

'Yes, Miss Ranger.'

As the English teacher chatted on, Elizabeth was staring at Jake's spellings which were on top of the batch in her hand. Twenty words were written down. Eighteen had red ticks by them and two had been marked with a red cross.

'. . . I'm afraid, Jake,' the teacher was saying, with a humorous smile, 'that SIGN and RESIGN become two completely different words when you leave the Gs out. RESIN is something produced from sap. And SIN is something you commit when you forget your silent Gs!'

Everyone laughed.

But Elizabeth's scalp prickled as she gazed at Jake's spellings; at that word RESIN, with its cross beside it. Briefly, she shut her eyes, then opened them again.

'And I've made a mistake, too,' she realised. 'Jake didn't write those notes. He couldn't have done.'

For on yesterday's message, she was quite sure the word RESIGN had been spelt correctly.

9   *Elizabeth learns Jake's secret*

'How clever of you to remember, Elizabeth,' said Joan, when they discussed it together at dinner-time. 'I'd never have thought of it. Thank goodness you remembered the wording of this message and worked out that it couldn't be Jake. Only just in time. You were planning to rush off and accuse him!'

'You're the really wise one, Joan,' said Elizabeth, humbly. 'You warned me I was being hot-headed! I was too stubborn to listen.'

They were both staring at the second anonymous message, which she had collected from upstairs. WHY NOT RESIGN PLEASE, ELIZABETH? it ended and it was all spelt correctly. The message was written *before* today's spelling test. If Jake had looked up the spelling to write the message, he would hardly have forgotten it for an important test.

'Jake's always struggled with English,' mused Joan. 'That's why he's still in the second form. I couldn't quite imagine him putting pen to paper to write messages. Jake's style is just to say things straight out!'

'Yes,' nodded Elizabeth. She looked rueful. 'And he's certainly done that as far as I'm concerned. But it was wrong of me to leap to conclusions.'

It was a warm day. The girls were sitting beneath the weeping ash tree, in the school grounds. All the leaves had turned colour in the past week. They were starting to float down now, carpeting the grass around them. Elizabeth caught a fluttering leaf in her hands and examined it. She was thinking hard. She so loved it here at Whyteleafe School but it was horrid having an enemy. Who DID write those messages?

'If Jake isn't the enemy then I want to know who is, Joan!' she said, angrily.

The two girls discussed the mystery all

dinner hour. They badly wanted to solve it. They went through possible suspects, as real detectives would.

'We can be sure it's a boy, and we can be sure he's in the second form,' said Joan, softly. 'So that narrows it down.'

'Not very much though,' replied Elizabeth, ruefully. 'The first thing is to think of the motive. It's got to be somebody who hates the idea of there being two girl monitors, who thinks it's unfair. Somebody other than Jake.'

'What about Daniel?' suggested Joan, tentatively.

'Oh, surely not Daniel!' exclaimed Elizabeth, in dismay. He was a gentle, sensitive boy. 'I like Daniel! And I'm sure he likes me! Except . . .'

She broke off, remembering the wistful expression on Daniel's face last week, when she'd come from an MM. *Oh, they do sound fun!* he'd said. Under his gentle exterior, could Daniel secretly be regretting that he'd stood down after his few days as a monitor, to give Elizabeth her place back?

'I don't want to think it's Daniel, Joan!' she stated. 'Let's think of somebody else. In books, it's always the last person you suspect . . .' she laughed. 'Say, Julian, for instance . . .'

Even as Elizabeth spoke her friend's name out loud, her laughter faded on her lips and her heart gave a jolt.

'Julian!' she whispered. 'Is it possible? He has been quite cutting lately about my being a monitor!'

'Oh, that's just his usual teasing, Elizabeth! The reason he's so cool is because you're being nice to Patrick. You know how those two cousins hate each other!'

'But you don't understand, Joan. He thinks I'm being nice to Patrick only because I *am* a monitor!'

Is this a bad attack of the goody-goody-monitor-itis disease? he'd asked her.

'I see,' said Joan. Then she looked at her friend in surprise. What did Elizabeth mean by 'only'? What other reason could she have for being specially nice to Patrick? 'Perhaps you've been overdoing it, Elizabeth. I do believe Julian's a little jealous.'

Elizabeth rapidly changed the subject. It was more than she could bear to think of Julian being her enemy; far worse, even, than it being Daniel.

'We're being silly, Joan,' she declared. 'It couldn't possibly be Julian! Or Daniel, come to that. Let's think of some other people.'

After a while, the two girls came to the most obvious conclusion. The message writer was probably one of the gang of boys who admired Jake. Martin, or Kenneth, or John McTavish . . .

'They're probably all in it together,' decided Joan.

But Elizabeth didn't find that any comfort, either.

In the distance, the bell went for afternoon lessons. As the two girls got to their feet and walked slowly back to school, Elizabeth looked thoughtful.

'Perhaps it doesn't matter *who's* writing the

messages, Joan,' she sighed. 'The fact is, I've made a mess of being a monitor. I shouldn't have told tales on Jake. And I shouldn't have allowed myself to get wound up and tried to stop the boys' pillow fights in the way I did. I'm no use as a monitor, if half the boys in the class don't respect me. Perhaps I'd *better* do as the note suggests. Offer to resign.'

'You can't do that, Elizabeth,' said Joan, giving her a sidelong glance. 'You can't give in to anonymous messages.'

'I'm in disgrace, anyway,' the Naughtiest Girl pointed out. 'Don't forget that Thomas is going to deal with me at the next MM! That's what Mr Leslie said. I may have no choice in the matter. I may be asked to resign, anyway!'

It was a horrid thought.

'We will just have to see about that, Elizabeth,' replied Joan kindly. 'Won't we?'

In spite of her own troubles, Elizabeth began to feel very worried over the next few days about a member of her class.

She had a growing sense of there being something seriously wrong with Jake.

Nobody else noticed much but Elizabeth found herself keeping a watchful eye on him. She was sure it was connected with the forthcoming hockey match against Milford Grange. She believed he might be dreading it with a sickening fear.

At first she thought it was her imagination, her own guilty conscience at work. But as each day passed, and the match drew inexorably nearer, she was sure that the big boy was becoming more and more desperate.

'Why don't you want to talk about the big match, Jake?' she heard his friend Kenneth ask him, peevishly. 'Why aren't you bothering to practise?'

'My hockey stick will have to do the talking,' Jake had snapped in reply. 'When it needs to!'

He seemed to be avoiding the other boys and they tactfully left him alone.

'He seems a bit tense about the match,' Martin commented. 'I suppose it's because he hasn't played since last season.'

'Jake? Tense about a hockey match?' scoffed John. 'It's school work getting him down, I expect!'

On Friday evening, at the school Meeting, Elizabeth watched Jake from her vantage point on the platform. She thought how glum he looked, wrapped in his own thoughts. He seemed to take no interest at all when the head boy and girl dealt with the matter of the pillow fights in Room 17.

'As the culprits have owned up, we've decided to let them off lightly,' announced Thomas, while Emma wrote it all down in the school's Big Book. 'They must sleep without pillows for a whole week. That will help them to remember that it is thoughtless to keep other boys awake at nights! After next week, their pillows will be returned to them.'

Even as Elizabeth sat there wondering what her own punishment was going to be, at next week's MM, she noticed that Jake had suddenly gone very pale.

'Finally, we hope you will all turn out and cheer the school hockey team tomorrow morning,' Thomas was saying. 'Milford Grange will be here at eleven o'clock and they are bringing two coachloads of supporters. I am sure you will all be very pleased to know that Jake is fully fit again and is now back in the Whyteleafe team. We are sure he plans to shoot plenty of goals for us tomorrow! Right, everyone. You are dismissed.'

There was laughter and cheers and the sound of benches scraping back. The Meeting was over! The boys and girls were all looking forward to the weekend.

Watching closely, Elizabeth saw Jake rise to his feet and sway slightly. She thought for a moment that he was going to faint. Then he hurried from the hall.

'Jake is terrified of tomorrow's match!' she realized. 'I'm positive now. The very thought of it seems to be making him ill. And it's all my fault! I'm the person who's put him in this position. I think I may have done a dreadful thing!'

Elizabeth hurried down off the platform. Her heart was beating fast. She could not begin to understand what was wrong with Jake, nor why he had been going to such extraordinary lengths to get out of playing hockey for Whyteleafe. But she was racked with guilt to see his suffering.

'I've got to catch up with him and tell him how sorry I am!' she decided. 'I don't care how rude he is to me, I've got to tell him I'm sorry and ask him to forgive me. Oh, what is wrong with him? I do wish there were some way I could make him feel better!'

She raced outside on to the lawn, just in time to see Jake disappearing in the direction of the school gardens. She hurried in pursuit.

When she got there, she saw him sitting quite alone on the wooden bench by the big greenhouse.

The gardens were silent and very still, with no breath of wind today. The rows of runner beans stood like withered green wigwams, their crop near its end. A blackbird rustled in the nearby yew hedge.

Elizabeth's warm heart ached with pity to see the big boy sitting on the bench, doubled up as though in pain. She tiptoed towards him. He was making little moaning sounds.

'Jake!' she whispered.

He raised his head. His eyes looked red.

'Elizabeth!' he gasped in surprise. 'What are you doing here? Please go away. I have such terrible stomach cramps. I can't bear anyone to see me like this, least of all a girl. Please go away – and don't tell anybody you've seen me in such a state!'

'I will NOT go away, Jake!' Elizabeth came and sat beside him and placed an arm round his big shoulders. 'I have come to ask your forgiveness. I know I have done something terrible, giving you away. And now you are scared to play in the match tomorrow. *I* can't bear it to see how scared you are.'

'You've guessed?' asked Jake, in alarm.

He buried his face in his hands. Elizabeth patted his heaving back, trying to soothe him.

'I can't bear it that a girl should see me like this,' he moaned.

Elizabeth continued to pat his back, gently.

'Please tell me what's wrong, Jake,' she begged. 'I promise on my honour that I'll keep your secret. But I'm so worried about you. I will cry *myself* if you don't tell me what's wrong!'

'I am so very, very scared, Elizabeth,' the boy blurted out. 'I am so frightened that the same thing could happen again.'

'What, Jake?' she prompted him gently, almost in tears herself.

He raised his head and gazed at her. He saw the anguished expression on her face and knew that, in this moment, she was living through his anguish with him. What a fine girl she was, he realized. He suddenly felt sure that he could trust her.

'A month ago, Elizabeth, I nearly blinded somebody,' he stated. 'The person I admire most in all the world. My coach, Henry Hill. Since my father died, he has been like a dad to me! He used to play hockey for England and he's coached me since I was a little boy. But I nearly blinded him. It was touch and go! He's only just come out of hospital.'

'What a terrible thing to happen!' gasped Elizabeth. 'Jake, please tell me the whole story. It will make you feel a little better to talk about it, even if it's only to me.'

At last Jake's strange behaviour began to make sense as he explained that, on the last day of the summer holidays, he'd played in a match for his home town hockey club. The club's non-playing captain was Henry Hill, a former England international, the man whom Jake so loved and admired. He had coached Jake for years, convinced that the boy would himself play for his country one day. His own playing days were over but because the team was one short that day, Henry had stepped in at short notice to fill the gap.

It had been a dramatic and closely-fought

contest but then had come disaster. A hard-struck ball by Jake had flown off at an angle and the ball had caught Henry in the eye with great force. An ambulance had been called and he'd been rushed to hospital. Only an emergency operation had saved the sight in his left eye.

'It was the most terrible day of my life,' Jake confessed. 'I will never be able to forget it. Henry's cries of pain . . . the ambulance wailing . . . then waiting all afternoon for some news from the hospital . . . I still have bad dreams about it. I really *did* hurt my ankle that day. It was just a slight sprain and my mother bandaged it up for me. Then, when I got back to school, it gave me an idea. I desperately wanted to give myself time! To try to get over what had happened . . .'

'And you didn't want to explain things to Mr Warlow, then?' ventured Elizabeth.

'No! He would have told me to put this behind me! He would have tried to rush me. And now, I *have* been rushed and the terrible thing is that I *can't* put this behind me, Elizabeth. I will never put it behind me! It is cowardly of me but I have completely lost my nerve. It could happen again, at any time! It could be something worse next time. Please don't tell anybody about this, Elizabeth. You are the only person who need ever know what a coward I am. I will have to find some new excuse but . . .'

He buried his face in his hands again.

'I can't play in tomorrow's match. I just can't.'

Elizabeth touched his arm.

'You *must*, Jake,' she whispered. 'You really must, you know. There's somebody you haven't been thinking about in all this.'

He looked at her in surprise.

'Who?'

'Henry, of course. You say he has coached you all this time and believes you will play for your country one day. The accident was a terrible thing but a younger person would have been able to react more quickly and dodge that flying ball. Henry shouldn't have been playing! But now, having given him one kind of pain, you are planning to make it much worse. You have been his life's work and now you are going to destroy all his dreams for you.'

Jake fell silent.

'I hadn't looked at it like that,' he said, at last.

Elizabeth remembered the time that she had fallen badly from her pony. Her governess had forced her instantly to remount. *The longer you leave it, Elizabeth, the more frightened you will be* she had told the little girl.

'You must play tomorrow, Jake,' she pleaded. 'For Henry's sake you must try to overcome your fears as quickly as possible and get back to playing a hard match once again. Please promise that you will try to overcome your terror.'

'I can't promise, Elizabeth,' Jake said, in despair. 'I am so very, very scared about it. Let me just sit here on my own for a while and think things over.'

'Yes, Jake.' Elizabeth rose to her feet. 'And your secret is safe with me. But will you at least promise me something else?'

'What's that, Elizabeth?'

'Ask if you can use the school telephone this evening! Telephone your coach, for he would be pleased to hear from you. And ask his opinion of what he thinks you should do.'

Leaving Jake deep in thought, she tiptoed away.

And the following morning Jake did, indeed, turn out for the match against Milford Grange. His jaw was clenched and his face pale as he ran out on to the pitch with the rest of the Whyteleafe first eleven.

Two people cheered him even louder than the rest. One of them was Elizabeth. The other was a man on the opposite side of the field who had just arrived with his wife. He had a large dressing over one eye, held securely in place by special bandages.

'That's my boy, Jake!' he called out loudly, raising both fists high.

After last night's telephone call, Henry Hill had asked his wife to drive him the thirty miles from their home town, so that he could watch Jake's match.

Jake made a nervous, even tentative, start but as the pace hotted up he began to get into his stride. He ran here, there and everywhere, tackling fiercely, soon caught up in the excitement of the hard-fought game. By the end of the match Whyteleafe had won 6–4 and Jake had scored five of the six goals!

As he walked off the pitch, Henry Hill came striding across to shake his hand.

'That was marvellous, Jake.' His face was shining and so was Jake's. 'I'm very proud of you, my boy. Keep it up. What a tonic for a poor sick invalid!'

'I've got to drag Henry away, Jake,' apologized Mrs Hill, tugging at her husband's arm. 'We're due at the hospital. The bandages come off today. Isn't that good news? I'm hoping the dear man has seen sense at last. I've told him to face the fact that his glory days are behind him. I hope that's going to be his last game!'

'It is. It is. But Jake's got all his glory days ahead of him. I'm so proud of you, my boy!' the man repeated, as he pumped Jake's hand and slapped him on the back. 'Good luck! See you at half-term!'

Jake watched his coach walk away. He was overcome with emotion.

Some of his classmates came racing over then and tried to close in on him. Martin, Kenneth, John . . . they were all very excited.

'Was that your famous coach, Jake?'

'Was that Henry Hill?'

But Jake strode away from them.

'Where's Elizabeth?' he demanded. 'Where's our famous monitor? That's who I want to see right now.'

To everybody's surprise, when he found Elizabeth he lifted her clean off the ground and swung her up on to his shoulders.

'Thank you, Elizabeth! You're the best monitor in the school! If anybody says any different, tell them to come and see me!'

They second form boys all looked at one another in amazement.

'What's Elizabeth done, then?' asked Kenneth.

'Given me my nerve back, that's what she's done!' Jake informed them. He was not ashamed to admit it to anyone now. 'I'll tell you the whole story later!'

Julian and Joan were surprised to see Jake parading round the hockey pitch with Elizabeth perched up high on his shoulders. He wanted her to share in his glory. She was laughing and waving to everybody. Some of the boys were cheering her!

'What's the Naughtiest Girl been up to now?' wondered Julian.

The story of how Elizabeth had helped Jake soon spread around the school. There were no more anonymous messages after that.

But the Monitors' Meeting still lay ahead.

10 *A mystery still unsolved*

'It was a reckless thing to do, Elizabeth. You had no business charging into the boys' quarters at night and encouraging some of your friends to join you! You must have known you were breaking a strict school rule,' said Thomas. 'That is hardly a sensible way for a monitor to deal with others who are breaking rules. By breaking one herself!'

The next MM was taking place. Silent and ashamed, Elizabeth sat next to Joan on the bench in the cosy little study. The moment of reckoning had come at last, the moment she had been dreading.

'You will never live down your Naughtiest Girl nickname if you do things like this, Elizabeth,' Emma pointed out. 'Because you are a monitor, we have spared you the shame of discussing this at the weekly Meeting. But it cannot go unpunished.'

'We understand that you were provoked,' went on Thomas, as the rest of the monitors listened with interest. 'Joan has told us that you were being teased and receiving anonymous messages from boys who appeared to think it unfair that your class has two girl monitors. They should have thought of that before, when they held the election! So Emma and I have decided on quite a modest punishment. You and your four friends must all go to bed one hour earlier for the next seven days. Do the other monitors think that sounds fair?'

There were murmurs of agreement from everyone. They all liked the Naughtiest Girl. She did crazy things sometimes but she had a very warm heart. They had all heard the story about Jake by now.

How marvellous that Joan had been and spoken up for her, thought Elizabeth. She felt herself going weak at the knees. She had got off lightly! What a relief! And what a relief it would be to give the good news to Jenny, Kathleen, Belinda and Tessa. She had felt guilty about leading them into trouble. She was sure they would not mind having to go to bed early for a few nights, any more than she did.

But just as her heart began to lighten, Emma spoke again.

'However, this whole situation has raised an important issue. Tom and I have had a long talk about it and we've talked it over with Joan, too. There *are* a lot of boys in Form 2. We feel that perhaps a mistake *was* made in appointing two girl monitors. What do you think, Elizabeth?'

'I – I—'

Elizabeth's spirits plunged. So she was going to be asked to resign, after all!

'If the form had had a boy monitor in office, some problems might have been avoided,' Thomas observed. 'For example, Jake is a big boy who prides himself on his physical strength. It was extremely difficult for him to confess to a girl how very frightened he felt. He might have found it easier to talk to another boy. It's just possible. And a boy monitor would certainly have ensured that the pillow-fighting craze was nipped in the bud.'

'Yes,' agreed Elizabeth. She steeled herself. 'If you want me to stand down then, I will quite understand . . .'

'Oh, Elizabeth, of course not!' exclaimed Joan. 'Not you – me!'

'Yes, cheer up, Elizabeth!' smiled Emma. 'Joan has already offered us her resignation. She feels that she has had a very long stint as monitor, whereas you have only just started. Even more important, she is finding that being a monitor is starting to clash with her swimming commitments. She has assured me that she will be perfectly happy to make way for a boy and she believes this is necessary.'

'Joan!' whispered Elizabeth, in surprise. 'Is this true? And is it true that you are going to be quite happy about it?'

'Perfectly true!' replied her friend. 'And perfectly happy!'

After further discussion it was agreed that Joan would stand down as monitor at the end of the next school Meeting. And after that, the second form boys could elect a monitor from amongst their number in time for the last Meeting before half-term.

Towards the end of the MM, the head boy and girl asked anxiously if any more citations had been handed in for the William and Rita Award.

There were three this week.

They all agreed that one of them was outstanding and should go on the shortlist. Elizabeth was very pleased about that. For it was one that Elizabeth herself had written out on the special form. Joan had read it beautifully.

'Won't it be lovely if our citation wins the award, Joan?' she said, as they walked into tea together. 'What an honour for the second form!'

'What's that?' asked Patrick in alarm, for he was just behind them.

'Don't worry, Patrick!' Elizabeth turned round and smiled at him. 'You shouldn't eavesdrop. But you can relax now. Something else has come up, so you're quite safe!'

'Whatever was that about?' asked Joan, looking puzzled as she watched Patrick stroll on past them, whistling softly.

'Oh, nothing, Joan,' Elizabeth replied quickly.

She smiled to herself. Dear Patrick. He could sleep easily in his bed at nights. Perhaps one day she would be able to persuade him to be nominated, in time for a future award. But there was no hurry now.

She was so pleased that she was going to be able to continue as a monitor. Joan really did not want to be one any more. But she was going to miss her. It had been so wonderful having a best friend as the other monitor, somebody to talk over the MMs with, to their heart's content. Who would the new monitor be? she wondered. Who would the boys elect? She would find out soon enough. She hoped it would be somebody she liked.

The one small irritation was the matter of those anonymous messages. The person who'd written them had in part got his way! Although he'd not succeeded in getting rid of Elizabeth as a monitor, there *was* going to be a boy monitor, which would no doubt please him. It was annoying to think of her enemy being pleased.

Who had written the notes? Would she ever find out?

It was a mystery still unsolved.

11 *Julian springs a huge surprise*

Truth will always out and the truth about the enemy came out in an amazing way. It was the last person that Elizabeth suspected. It came out at the next Meeting.

All the usual weekly business had been conducted. And then Emma announced that Joan would be resigning as a monitor.

'There are a lot of boys in the second form this year. It has been decided by all concerned that it would be better to have one boy and one girl monitor. We shall be asking the second form boys to elect their representative at next week's Meeting, ready for the second half of term. In the meantime could we all give Joan a round of applause, please, for her long and distinguished service to the second form.'

There was prolonged applause for Joan.

Some of the boys and girls cheered and stamped their feet, as well. Sitting proudly next to her on the platform, Elizabeth glanced at her friend affectionately. How she was going to miss the great adventure of their being monitors together! But Joan had set her heart on getting strong and fit enough to be a member of Miss Thomas's swimming team and her time was going to be rationed now.

As the applause died away, the children all started chattering. They thought that the Meeting was over. But Thomas rapped the table sharply with the little gavel.

'Silence, please. There is one more matter to attend to. I'll let Emma do the talking.'

The head girl stood up.

'Somewhere in this hall, there is a boy who broke a school rule and went to the village on his own, two or three weeks ago,' she stated. 'It was very wrong of him for the rule is a very strict one. But just this once he will not be punished. I can see you are all wondering why,' she added, for a great hush had fallen over the hall. 'Well, I can tell you why. A woman has been to see us today. She brought this with her.'

Lying on the table, next to the school Book, was a large cardboard box. Emma took something out of the box. With a dramatic flourish she held it up for the whole school to see.

It was a giant box of chocolates.

All the children gasped with excitement. What was coming next? Elizabeth stiffened. She stared down into the hall to the second form benches. Patrick was sitting there, a slow pallor creeping up his cheeks.

'With no thought of danger to himself, this boy rushed into the road and saved the woman's child from being run over. The child was walking straight into the path of an oncoming car and would no doubt have been injured – or worse – without this boy's intervention. However he hurried away without waiting to be thanked.'

Emma paused for breath.

'After that, the woman saw the boy on a more recent occasion. The child recognized him at once. On this occasion the mother managed quickly to thank him but once again he hurried off. She feels he deserves some proper reward and she has asked that he be presented with this box of chocolates in front of the whole school. So, Thomas and I would now like our shy hero to stand up and make himself known. Who is he, please?'

The pupils were enthralled. They started whispering and nudging one another, gazing all round the hall. Who would stand up?

Elizabeth was staring at Patrick in deep fascination. What was going to happen now? In spite of all his efforts to keep his heroism a secret, it was going to be impossible for him to hide it now!

Patrick seemed to be frozen to the bench. His eyes were darting this way and that. Once or twice he craned his neck to look round at the benches behind him.

'He's still trying to keep it secret, even now!'

thought Elizabeth. 'He's looking round, like everybody else. Pretending that he's waiting to see who's going to stand up.'

Emma stood there, holding the chocolates. The seconds ticked by. And Patrick still sat there, gazing all round. Two or three places along on the bench, Julian scratched his head and looked puzzled. Other children were talking in low voices. It was beginning to get embarrassing.

'Would the boy please stand up?' repeated Emma, colouring a little.

Still no one did so. Then Thomas lost patience.

He banged the gavel hard on the table.

'Would the boy in question stand up at once, please?' he said. 'That's an order.'

Elizabeth managed to catch Patrick's eye. And then – slowly, very slowly, Patrick rose to his feet, his face drained of colour. But then Elizabeth gave a little gasp. For something very strange was happening. At exactly the same moment, Julian was slowly rising, too!

Languidly, his hands in his pockets.

Both boys were standing up together!

'Was this child a girl and did she have red hair, by any chance?' enquired Julian.

'Yes, she was a girl. And her mother certainly has red hair,' replied Thomas. 'Why, do you know something about it? Please take your hands out of your pockets, Julian.'

With Patrick now standing frozen in horror, a little further along the same bench, Julian took his hands out of his pockets and grinned.

'I think it must have been me, then. I'm afraid I'd forgotten all about it. What perplexed me was Emma saying the boy was seen in the village a second time. You see I haven't been down again since the other week when that kid ran in the road! But now, I realize –' he turned and smiled at Patrick with a scornful gleam in his eye '– that she could have confused me with somebody else.'

Patrick looked as though he wished the ground would swallow him up.

Slowly, he subsided back down on to the bench.

Elizabeth gazed from one cousin to the other, in shock. She was reminded how alike they looked, with their matted black hair and brilliant green eyes! How easy it would have been for the child to make her mistake!

It was not Patrick who'd performed the brave deed at all. It was Julian! And now Julian was strolling up to the platform and being presented with the chocolates! And the whole school was clapping and cheering him!

While, down below, Patrick sat miserably hunched on the bench.

And when all the excitement had died down, Thomas held his hand up for silence one last time. He asked Patrick to get to his feet.

'Don't ever try to do that again,' he told him, shaming him in front of the whole school. 'Of all the kinds of stealing there are, to try to steal another person's glory is the most despicable.'

The head boy was angry enough. But

Elizabeth's own anger put even his in the shade. She could hardly wait to vent her feelings.

'You complete and absolute worm!' she told Patrick afterwards, dragging him outside on to the terrace. 'No wonder you didn't want me to name you for the William and Rita Award! If I'd done that, the person who had really performed the brave deed would soon have had something to say about it, wouldn't they? How could you bear to let me think you were a hero all this time? You have made an absolute fool of me. I hate you!'

'Please don't hate me, Elizabeth,' begged Patrick. 'You never gave me the chance to explain that the little girl had made a mistake. You really didn't! I had no idea who'd really saved her. I hadn't a clue. But it was just so thrilling to have you looking up to me and liking me for a change! I would have explained straight away but you never gave me the chance, Elizabeth! And after that I thought, what harm could it possibly do anyone else, the child making a silly mistake and you thinking it was me?'

Elizabeth's anger began to subside as she saw how distressed the boy was. She also realized that he was telling the truth. She'd given him almost no chance at all to explain there'd been a mistake! She'd made such a fuss of him at the time. It must have been awkward for him.

'It all seemed so simple at first,' Patrick confessed. 'It was so nice that you liked me. And the woman seemed really pleased to have someone to thank! I thought nothing more would come of it. But then it was dreadful when this business of the Award came up and you wanted to put my name forward! I longed to make a clean breast of things but when you told me that you'd given up your place in the table-tennis team, I was finished! That was the worst thing of all, Elizabeth. After that, I became desperate that the truth should never, ever come out. I even wrote those silly notes—'

'YOU wrote the notes, Patrick?' gasped Elizabeth. 'YOU were the enemy? I thought of everyone else but I never thought of you!'

'I'm not an enemy, Elizabeth. But I knew that as long as you kept on going to those MMs of yours, sooner or later you'd have blurted something out about my so-called brave deed. I know what you're like! So I was hoping, with some of the boys making trouble for you anyway, that you might get fed up with being a monitor.'

'I see.'

Elizabeth frowned. She didn't know whether to be angry or amused. For she was relieved to discover that she did not have a real enemy.

'Patrick, I think you are pathetic!' she added.

'Well, I really *did* think it was unfair having two girl monitors,' Patrick objected. 'I've always said that.'

Elizabeth thought back over all the time she'd known Patrick.

It was true! He had often said it. In fact he didn't really approve of the school having girls in it, at all!

How silly of her not to have remembered that.

'Well, there's going to be a boy monitor anyway,' she pointed out.

'Yes,' replied Patrick smugly. 'Thomas and Emma seem to agree with me on that.'

Elizabeth turned on her heel. Julian had appeared on the terrace, looking for her. She called back to Patrick, over her shoulder.

'I only hope it's not you, Patrick!'

Julian grinned.

'Hello, Elizabeth. Been giving my cousin a telling-off about something? Here, have a chocolate. They're delicious.'

It was the last Meeting before half-term. A gleaming little silver trophy stood on the head boy and girl's table. The very first William and Rita Award was about to be announced.

'We ended up with four citations on the shortlist,' Thomas was telling the assembled school, 'of which two were quite outstanding. Miss Belle and Miss Best and Emma and I had a very difficult job deciding between them. One was for Julian Holland, signed by several boys in his class. For his brave action in saving the little girl from being run over. The other was for Jake Johnson, signed by Elizabeth Allen, for his courage in overcoming a personal crisis.'

While the whole school hung on to his words, Thomas paused for maximum effect.

'Which one were we to choose? Which boy had shown the greater courage? As we talked it over, we came to realize that Julian's fearless deed had come as second nature to him. It was truly fearless for he had felt no fear. He saw the child in danger and instantly took action. We are very proud of him for that. But his brave deed meant so little to him that he had some difficulty in remembering it afterwards.

'Jake, on the other hand, and I know he does not mind us telling you this now, felt absolute terror at the thought of playing hockey again after inflicting a grave injury on someone he loved and admired. Yet somehow he faced that fear and fought it and in the end, he overcame it.

'Fearlessness and courage are not the same thing. A high form of courage is to know real fear – and then to overcome it. The school therefore takes great pride in giving the very first William and Rita Award to – Jake Johnson.'

The school clapped and cheered as the gentle giant of a boy shambled up on the platform and took the little silver trophy from Emma's outstretched hand. He clutched it proudly and shot Elizabeth an embarrassed smile. She was sitting behind Emma on the platform, clapping so hard that her palms stung.

As the Meeting broke up, she turned to the boy sitting next to her.

'A lot of the boys wanted you to have the Award, Julian, but I think the Beauty and the Beast and Thomas and Emma have all made the right decision, don't you?'

'Most definitely,' agreed Julian.

'And at least the boys elected you as

monitor!' she said, with a happy sigh.

It was nice to have Julian sitting next to her on the platform.

She would still have a friend as her fellow monitor, after all. A truly marvellous friend. Poor Patrick! But what fun it was going to be from now on, she and Julian being monitors together!

'Yes, I'm a monitor,' replied Julian, with a cheerful grin. 'I still can't believe it and as a matter of fact, Elizabeth, I don't know how I'm going to manage it. But for your sake, I suppose I'd better try.'

'You suppose right, Julian,' she laughed.

If you can't wait
to read more about
The
Naughtiest Girl,
then turn over for
the beginning of her
next adventure...

The Naughtiest
Girl in the
school

1 *The naughty spoilt girl*

'You'll have to go to school, Elizabeth!' said Mrs Allen. 'I think your governess is quite right. You are spoilt and naughty, and although Daddy and I were going to leave you here with Miss Scott when we went away, I think it would be better for you to go to school.'

Elizabeth stared at her mother in dismay. What, leave her home? And her pony and her dog? Go and be with a lot of children she would hate? Oh no, she wouldn't go!

'I'll be good with Miss Scott,' she said.

'You've said that before,' said her mother. 'Miss Scott says she can't stay with you any longer. Elizabeth, is it true that you put earwigs in her bed last night?'

Elizabeth giggled. 'Yes,' she said. 'Miss Scott

is so frightened of them! It's silly to be afraid of earwigs, isn't it?'

'It is much sillier to put them into somebody's bed,' said Mrs Allen sternly. 'You have been spoilt, and you think you can do what you like! You are an only child, and we love you so much, Daddy and I, that I think we have given you too many lovely things, and allowed you too much freedom.'

'Mummy, if you send me to school, I shall be so naughty there that they'll send me back home again,' said Elizabeth, shaking her curls back. She was a pretty girl with laughing blue eyes and dark brown curls. All her life she had done as she liked. Six governesses had come and gone, but not one of them had been able to make Elizabeth obedient or good-mannered!

'You can be such a nice little girl!' they had all said to her, 'but all you think of is getting into mischief and being rude about it!'

And now when she said that she would be so naughty at school that they would have to send her home, her mother looked at her in despair. She loved Elizabeth very much, and wanted her to be happy – but how could she be happy if she did not learn to be as other children were?

'You have been alone too much, Elizabeth,' she said. 'You should have had other children to play with and to work with.'

'I don't like other children!' said Elizabeth sulkily. It was quite true – she didn't like boys and girls at all! They were shocked at her mischief and rude ways, and when they said they wouldn't join in her naughtiness, she laughed at them and said they were babies. Then they told her what they thought of her, and Elizabeth didn't like it.

So now the thought of going away to school and living with other boys and girls made Elizabeth feel dreadful!

'Please don't send me,' she begged. 'I really will be good at home.'

'No, Elizabeth,' said her mother. 'Daddy and I *must* go away for a whole year, and as Miss Scott won't stay, and we could not expect to find another governess quickly before we go, it is best you should go to school. You have a good brain and you should be able to do your work well and get to the top of the form. Then we shall be proud of you.'

'I shan't work at all,' said Elizabeth, pouting. 'I won't work a bit, and they'll think I'm so stupid they won't keep me!'

'Well, Elizabeth, if you want to make things difficult for yourself, you'll have to,' said Mother, getting up. 'We have written to Miss Belle and Miss Best, who run Whyteleafe School, and they are willing to take you next week, when the new term begins. Miss Scott will get all your things ready. Please help her all you can.'

Elizabeth was very angry and upset. She didn't want to go to school. She hated everybody, especially silly children! Miss Scott was horrid to say she wouldn't stay. Suddenly Elizabeth wondered if she *would* stay, if she asked her very, very nicely!

She ran to find her governess. Miss Scott

was busy sewing Elizabeth's name on to a pile of brown stockings.

'Are these new stockings?' asked Elizabeth, in surprise. 'I don't wear stockings! I wear socks!'

'You have to wear stockings at Whyteleafe School,' said Miss Scott. Elizabeth stared at the pile, and then she suddenly put her arms round Miss Scott's neck.

'Miss Scott!' she said. 'Stay with me! I know I'm sometimes naughty, but I don't want you to go.'

'What you *really* mean is that you don't want to go to school,' said Miss Scott. 'I suppose Mother's been telling you?'

'Yes, she has,' said Elizabeth. 'Miss Scott, I *won't* go to school!'

'Well, of course, if you're such a baby as to be afraid of doing what all other children do, then I've nothing more to say,' said Miss Scott, beginning to sew another name on a brown stocking.

Elizabeth stood up at once and stamped her

foot. 'Afraid!' she shouted. '*I'm* not afraid! Was I afraid when I fell off my pony? Was I afraid when our car crashed into the bank? Was I afraid when – when – when—'

'Don't shout at me, please, Elizabeth,' said Miss Scott. 'I think you are afraid to go to school and mix with obedient, well-mannered, hard-working children who are not spoilt as you are. You know quite well that you wouldn't get your own way, that you would have to share everything, instead of having things to yourself as you do now, and that you would have to be punctual, polite, and obedient. And you are afraid to go!'

'I'm not, I'm not, I'm not!' shouted Elizabeth. 'I shall go! But I shall be so naughty and lazy that they won't keep me, and then I'll come back home! And you'll have to look after me again, so there!'

'My dear Elizabeth, I shan't be here,' said Miss Scott, taking another stocking. 'I am going to another family, where I shall have two little boys to teach. I am going the day you go to school. So you can't come back home because I shan't be here, your father and mother will be away, and the house will be shut up!'

Elizabeth burst into tears. She sobbed so loudly that Miss Scott, who was really fond of the spoilt, naughty girl, put her arms round her and comforted her.

'Now don't be silly,' she said. 'Most children simply *love* school. It's great fun. You play games, you go for walks, all together, you have the most lovely lessons, and you will make such a lot of friends. You have no friends now, and it is a dreadful thing not to have a single friend. You are very lucky.'

'I'm not,' wept Elizabeth. 'Nobody loves me. I'm very unhappy.'

'The trouble is that people have loved you too much,' said Miss Scott. 'You are pretty, and merry, and rich, so you have been spoilt. People like the way you look, the way you smile, and your pretty clothes so they fuss you, and pet you, and spoil you, instead of treating you like an ordinary child. But it isn't enough to have a pretty face and a merry smile – you must have a good heart too.'

Nobody had spoken to Elizabeth like this before, and the little girl was astonished. 'I *have* got a good heart,' she said, tossing her curls back again.

'Well, you don't show it much!' said Miss Scott. 'Now run away, please, because I've got to count all these stockings, and then mark your new vests and bodices.'

Elizabeth looked at the pile of stockings. She hated them. Nasty brown things! She wouldn't wear them! She'd take her socks to school and wear *those* if she wanted to! Miss Scott turned to a chest of drawers and began to take out some vests. Elizabeth picked up two brown stockings and pinned them toe to toe. Then she tiptoed to Miss Scott and neatly and quietly pinned them to her skirt.

She skipped out of the room, giggling. Miss Scott carried the vests to the table. She began to count the stockings. There should be six pairs.

'One – two – three – four – five,' she counted.
'Five. Dear me – where's the sixth?'

She looked on the floor. She looked on the
chair. She was really vexed. She counted the
pile again. Then she went to the door and
looked for Elizabeth. The little girl was pulling
something out of a cupboard on the landing.

'Elizabeth!' called Miss Scott sharply, 'have
you got a pair of brown stockings?'

'No, Miss Scott,' said Elizabeth, making her
eyes look round and surprised. 'Why?'

'Because a pair is missing,' said Miss Scott.
'Did you take them out of this room?'

'No, really, Miss Scott,' said Elizabeth
truthfully, trying not to laugh as she caught
sight of the stockings swinging at Miss Scott's
back. 'I'm sure all the stockings are in the room,
Miss Scott, really!'

'Then perhaps your mother has a pair,' said
Miss Scott. 'I'll go and ask her.'

Off marched the governess down the
landing, the pinned brown stockings trailing
behind her like a tail. Elizabeth put her head

into the cupboard and squealed with laughter. Miss Scott went into her mother's room.

'Excuse me, Mrs Allen,' she said, 'but have you one of Elizabeth's new pairs of stockings? I've only five pairs.'

'No, I gave you them all,' said Mrs Allen, surprised. 'They must be together. Perhaps you have dropped them somewhere.'

Miss Scott turned to go, and Mrs Allen caught sight of the brown stockings following Miss Scott. She looked at them in astonishment.

'Wait, Miss Scott,' she said. 'What's this!' She went to Miss Scott, and unpinned the stockings. The governess looked at Mrs Allen.

'Elizabeth, of course!' she said.

'Yes, Elizabeth!' said Mrs Allen. 'Always in mischief. I really never knew such a child in my life. It is high time she went to school. Don't you agree, Miss Scott?'

'I do,' said Miss Scott heartily. 'You will see a different and much nicer child when you come back home again, Mrs Allen!'

Elizabeth was passing by, and heard what

her mother and her governess were saying. She hit the door with the book she was carrying and shouted angrily.

'You won't see me any different, Mother, you won't, you won't! I'll be worse!'

'You couldn't be!' said Mrs Allen in despair. 'You really *couldn't* be worse!'